SPLITS AND TRANSITIONS

JAMES TARR

BOOKS

Vinci Books

vinci-books.com

Published by Vinci Books Ltd in 2025

1

Copyright © James Tarr 2020

The author has asserted their moral right to be identified as the author of this work in accordance with the Copyright, Designs and Patents Act 1988. This work is a work of fiction. Names, characters, places and incidents are the product of the author's imagination or are used fictitiously. Any resemblance to actual persons, living or dead, places and incidents is entirely coincidental.

All rights reserved. No part of this publication may be copied, reproduced, distributed, stored in any retrieval system, or transmitted in any form or by any means, including photocopying, recording, or other electronic or mechanical methods, nor used as a source for any form of machine learning including AI datasets, without the prior written permission of the publisher.

The publisher and the author have made every effort to obtain permissions for any third party material used in this book and to comply with copyright law. Any queries in this respect should be brought to the attention of the publisher and any omissions will be corrected in future editions.

A CIP catalogue record for this book is available from the British Library.

Paperback ISBN: 9781036701109

Printed and bound in Great Britain by Clays Ltd, Elcograf S.p.A.

By James Tarr

James Tarr Conspiracy Thrillers

Failure Drill

Splashback

Splits and Transitions

Whorl

Waiting for the Kick

Ghosts and Madmen

The Subsection

JUNE 2003

Chapter One

"I told you, I don't want you calling. Anything you want to say, you can say to my lawyer."

Her voice in my ear, as usual, sent a riot of emotions wildly bouncing around my head and heart. I stared down at the cup of coffee in front of me, today's copy of the Detroit Free Press next to it, and tried to find the right words.

After a slow, deep breath, I said, "I just wanted to talk."

"We've got nothing to talk about. If you weren't doing everything you could to stop it, we'd already be divorced. And we'd never have to talk again." Her bitterness held an accusation, and in truth she wasn't wrong. Michigan was a no-fault state when it came to divorce, and whether I contested it or not I couldn't stop it, although I'd been dragging it out as long as possible in the hope I could get Kelly to change her mind. The only thing that could have significantly slowed the process would have been the presence of minor children. And, to be honest, the fact that we didn't, currently, have a child was the main reason for the divorce.

I took another deep breath, trying to calm myself. "I've been…I'm…I did what you asked, I moved out—" I began.

"Only because I threatened to call the cops on you." Not that she was living in the house we'd shared either. She'd moved out less than a week after I had. Too many bad memories there. For both of us.

I blinked and tried to find my way back to that calm center I'd had before dialing the phone. "Why can't we just talk? I know you're hurting. I'm hurting too."

"I don't care if you're hurting!" she screamed in my ear. "You should be hurting! They're dead because of you."

"I didn't kill the dog or the baby!" I shouted back at her, then found I was talking to a dead line. And realized that a number of people sitting nearby were staring at me. Squeezing the phone hard enough for it to creak I glared at each one of them in turn until they looked away. Then I looked around the Starbucks, which was brand new and just half a mile from my office. Other than the two retirees I was the oldest person in the place. I was definitely the angriest, having caffeine and hate for lunch. As usual.

In a surprisingly adult move I resisted the urge to throw my cell phone across the room and instead tossed it onto the folded newspaper, atop the article I'd been reading, trying to slow my pulse. A glowing, feature-length front page obituary on Bernard Mitton, Detroit icon. Businessman and philanthropist, he got his start with a furniture store that he'd turned into a very successful Midwest chain—The Ottoman Empire. Always loved that name. Used the cash from that to start several other very successful businesses. Dead in the middle of a street, shot down during an attempted carjacking at age seventy-three. Both he and his aging trophy wife, who'd actually hired me once. What a waste. It didn't make my mood any better.

Splits and Transitions

There were half a dozen emails in my inbox when I came back from lunch, and a fresh fax in the machine. After skimming everything I grabbed the office phone and called Jerry Phillips. He answered his cell on the second ring.

"Yeah, I got another case in," I told him. "You available to work a surveillance tomorrow?

I'd known him for two years—been initially hired by his parents to find him, actually, and since then I'd seen a lot of drama with him and his friends. More than most people would ever believe, not that we were allowed to tell anyone. He'd graduated from Michigan State not quite two months earlier and been working for me while waiting for the job he wanted. I was going to miss him when he headed to FLETC (pronounced flet-see), the Federal Law Enforcement Training Centers in Georgia, where just about every federal law enforcement agent other than the FBI and DEA cadre were trained. He'd put in his application for the U.S. Marshals Service. Luckily, for me, the government's hiring process was horribly slow and inefficient, taking months, sometimes years to complete. Oddly enough, the USMS didn't polygraph its applicants which, in his case, was helpful. Very helpful.

"Morning? Yeah. Who's it for?" I could tell from the background noise he was driving.

"Uhhhh." I re-checked the paperwork. "MHC. Work comp. Where are you on your way to?"

"The gym." He coughed into the phone, then snorted. "MHC. Another hospital case? So we're watching a nurse who's out on carpal tunnel or a latex allergy. Waitwaitwait, they give you a description?"

"Ummmmm. Yeah. She's—"

"Let me guess. Five-two, two hundred pounds?"

My eyes scanned the paperwork. "Pretty close. A bit taller." I read through the descriptors. "A bit heavier."

"Okay, I take it back, she's got back or leg problems."

"Aren't you too young to be this cynical?" I checked. "Yep. Hip and knee."

I could hear him sigh. "You know, I can't believe how many of these so-called health professionals are just big fat giant pigs. The people you'd *think* would know better. Who do know better."

"Well, they work a lot of hours, and don't get much exercise," I said in their defense.

"You don't get fat by not exercising," he said sharply, "you get it by eating too goddamn much for the calories you're burning. There, look, I could write my own diet book, make a million dollars. I'll call it Shut Your Pie Hole."

"Oprah'd love you," I told him. "You're so sensitive. They're splurging for a two-man, so I'll e-mail you the address, and see you there at six." First goal of a work comp surveillance was to make sure the claimant wasn't working a second job while off work for the insured, so we usually started the first day at six a.m.

He must have heard something in my voice. "How you doing?" His concern was real. He knew my situation.

"Great. Living the dream. See you tomorrow." I hung up on him.

Just before four I heard the front door open and the click of high heels on the fancy laminate floor of my office. I was out of my chair and coming out from behind my desk when I heard the tentative "Hello?"

"Hi, can I help you?" I said from my office doorway.

"Are you Mr. Phault?"

"That'd be me."

She looked about twenty-five, pretty and thin, with curly blonde hair in a pile atop her head. She wore a short-sleeved white blouse unbuttoned dangerously low in front and a tight skirt that didn't come anywhere near her knees. In one hand was a small black clasp-purse, and she glanced around the office automatically. In her heels she was about five eleven, and was probably the best-looking person I'd ever had in my office. Other than me, of course.

"I got your name from the deputies down at the courthouse. I don't know if you can help me, or if I've even got a problem," she looked uncertain and a bit flustered. She paused and frowned.

I waved her into my office. "Come on in and sit down," I told her with a smile. I got settled behind the desk and she took the client chair in front of me, crossing her legs tightly at the knee. She tugged at the skirt to make sure it didn't ride too far up. Not that I was looking.

"What do you think you need a PI for?" I asked her.

She took a deep breath. "That's just it, I'm not sure if I do or not. Here, let me start at the beginning. I just moved here six months ago, from California. L.A., actually."

"Welcome to America," I said with a smile.

She looked at me strangely, not getting it at first, then gave me a wry grin. "Yeah, we're a bit out there. Oh, I'm Kerrie, Kerrie Edwards." We got back up and shook hands over my desk.

"John," I told her.

"Anyway, one of the reasons I moved here…" She frowned. "I had a stalker," she told me. "An ex-boyfriend. I had to get a restraining order against him and everything."

"He hurt you?" I asked.

She shook her head quickly. "No, he never laid a finger

on me, but he just became…obsessed, you know? He couldn't get over me after we broke up. God, that sounds conceited." She made a face.

I shook my head. "Lot of problems in the world caused by dudes who won't take no for an answer."

"Anyway, he wouldn't leave me alone. He'd send me flowers two or three times a week, call me ten times a day. I'd change my phone number, and three weeks later he was calling again, somehow he'd find it out. I'm pretty sure he was following me, too. I caught glimpses of his car, I think, a couple of times, but I could never say for sure. We were really close at one time, serious, but I was going through a rough spot in my life and he… Sorry," she stopped herself. "You don't need to hear my problems. I got the restraining order, and everything was fine for a week or so, then I saw him one night out my window, watching my apartment. This was like three o'clock in the morning, and I just got up to use the bathroom. I have no idea how long he'd been out there or anything. He was just staring."

"Creepy," I agreed.

"I called the cops," she told me, "but by the time they showed up he was gone. I kept an eye out for him, and didn't see him the next night, or the night after that, but then I saw him again. I called 911, but he took off. A couple of officers talked to him at work and he denied everything, said I was just trying to get back at him for dumping me."

"Of course."

"The police asked if I wanted to pursue it, try and get him for violating the order, but there weren't any witnesses, and Mike's one hell of a liar. I figured there was a better than even chance that the judge would believe him over me. So I came out here. I'd been wanting to make a change anyway."

"Michigan from L.A.? Detroit? That's a hell of a change."

"My mom lives out here," she told me. "And I just had a crappy receptionist job, it's not like I couldn't find something similar here. I'm trying to get my CPA, and once I saw most of my credits would transfer over I moved. I just packed my stuff into my car one day and took off, you know? I didn't tell anyone but a couple friends where I was going, just in case."

"And now?"

She made a face. "About a month ago I thought I saw his car again, here, following me. He drives this electric blue Mustang, I don't know, about an '88. It's souped up, with a loud exhaust. A couple of times I tried to turn around and follow it, see if it was him, but it just disappeared."

"So you've seen it more than once?"

She nodded. "I think I've seen him once or maybe twice a week for the past month."

That made me sit up. "Oh."

She shrugged. "I still don't know if it's him, the windows are tinted, and I've never seen the plate. But I think it is. I called my friends in L.A., and they checked his apartment. It's empty, and he quit his job. Nobody at the shop knows where he's working now. That doesn't mean he came all the way to Michigan after me, I know, but…."

"But it's got you worried."

She nodded nervously. "That's why I was at the courthouse. I was trying to get a restraining order against him. That's not what they call them here, they're…." She frowned, thinking.

"Personal Protection Orders," I told her.

"That's it. I went in front of a judge, but she told me I didn't have enough to get one issued. I couldn't say for sure it was even his car, or if it was him inside it. Or, if he's in this state, even where he lives. She sent me across the street to the Sheriff's Department."

I nodded. "They check to see if he was a resident?"

"Yeah. He doesn't have a Michigan driver's license, or any license plates registered to him here. They had no record of him on their computer. The judge said that part of getting a restraining order issued was that it had to be served on the person. I've got no address for him, no license plate, nothing. I might even be imagining the whole thing. The whole thing really freaked me out the first time, and just when I was starting to forget about it…."

"Well, I sure wouldn't fault you after the track record you've had with this guy," I told her. "Better to be safe than sorry. If he had a brown Taurus or something common like that I might be a little hesitant to make the call, but an electric blue eighties Mustang is a little different. Did he know your mom lives out here?"

"Yes."

I grabbed a legal pad from a drawer and jotted down some notes. "What I can do," I told her, "is run him on the computer, see what I can dig up."

"The police couldn't find any record of him anywhere."

"Apples and oranges," I assured her. "They ran him through the Secretary of State and LEIN, the Law Enforcement Information Network. That's driver's licenses, vehicle registration, traffic tickets, and criminal records. Do you have a Social Security number for him?"

"Yes, I've got everything," she said, starting to dig through her small purse. "From the first time, in California, for the restraining order. I typed it all out." She handed me several sheets of paper and I began unfolding them as I talked.

"This will make it a lot easier," I told her. "I can run him through a number of databases and search engines. Tax records, employment, phone bills, even utilities. Day-to-day life stuff. Chances are, if he's in Michigan, he'll turn up." I looked at the Xerox of his driver's license. The photo was small and a bit blurry.

"How much will that cost?" she asked me.

"Hundred bucks," I told her. "But if I find him here, you're going to have some decisions to make."

"What do you mean?"

"Even if you confirm he's in Michigan, you can't say for sure it was him following you. Unless something else happens, you still don't have enough for a PPO."

"Wouldn't the fact that he followed me here be enough?"

I shrugged. "You said he's a fast talker. He could say he didn't know you were here, that's he's only here because of a job, any number of things. Free country."

"What about the restraining order? It's still in effect."

"Are California restraining orders valid in Michigan? That's an actual question, because I don't know." I could see she didn't either. It was one more thing I'd have to look into. "Has he ever laid a hand on you? Ever physically threatened you?" She shook her head. "You want the good news or the bad news? Say he was caught red-handed doing something the California order prohibited, like appearing within your sight. Or closer than fifty feet or whatever the proscribed distance is, and it's just as valid here as an out-of-state warrant. You think anybody from California is going to fly out to Michigan to take him back there just to be charged? Is violation a misdemeanor or a felony?" I asked her.

She squinched her eyes up. "I think it depends."

"*You* don't even live there anymore," I told her. "Forget California. If he's here, the quickest way for you to get a PPO issued against him is to document him stalking you."

"But I told you, I couldn't tell—"

I shook my head. "Let's wait to worry about that until after we know something," I said. "But I'm not talking about sitting around waiting for something bad to happen," I explained. "It depends on how much money you'd be willing or able to spend, but there are a couple ways to go about it. Simplest, I think, would be to do surveillance on him. You show a judge an hour of video of him staring at your house or workplace, or I testify that I observed him following you home, and you won't have any problem getting a PPO."

"Oh, okay." She dug through her little purse again and withdrew some cash. She counted out a hundred dollars and handed it to me. "How long will it take you to do the search for him?" she asked me.

"I'll call you tomorrow," I told her, as I wrote out a receipt for the money. She gave me all her info and well as her current address, her mother's house which was in Troy not too far from my office.

"And tomorrow after we talk," I told her, "whether I find a trace of him or not, go to the Troy Police Department, and file what they call an 'information report'."

"What's that?"

"It's to let them know that something is going on. You may not have enough for a PPO, but going on record that you've got a concern will go a long way if there ever is a problem. Gets you on the scoreboard first. If the cops get a 911 call from your house, this report will pop up on their system, give them a heads up. And if you do see him," I told her, "don't wait, call 911."

Splits and Transitions

I leaned back in my chair and studied her long enough for her to start to get uncomfortable, then spoke. "Look, brutal honesty here. If this guy is so obsessed with you that he followed you all the way to Detroit from LA, in violation of one restraining order, one more piece of paper isn't going to make you any safer. Not in the real world. Keep a cell phone with you at all times, and get a can of pepper spray. Better yet, Michigan's a 'shall issue' state, and you've got a Michigan Driver's license, go get yourself a CCW and keep a gun in your car if you don't want to carry it on your person. You don't need a CCW if you keep it at the house."

She made a face and shook her head. "I don't like guns. I don't want to get a gun."

"Liking's got nothing to do with it," I told her. "It's a tool, same as a hammer or a screwdriver." I paused, and decided to make my point. I stood up. Even with the desk between us I towered over her. "I'm no freak of nature, and you're not a small woman, but I've got five inches and at least fifty pounds on you. I don't care if you're a black belt or have a can of pepper spray already in your hand, or even a knife, if I wanted to rape you or kill you, ninety-nine times out of a hundred there is no way you could stop me unless you had a gun. Period. And I'm old enough to be your father. Well, older brother." I sat back down, seeing from the look on her face that I'd scared the hell out of her.

"Sorry," I said, trying to sound like I meant it. "I've never been accused of subtlety or political correctness. It's just that I've seen too many bad things happen to good people, especially women. Bullies don't stop what they're doing if you ask them nicely."

She bit her lip. "I just don't think I could shoot him. He's never been violent."

I nodded. "And that's just fine. I wish there were more

people in the world who couldn't shoot other people. And until you're sure you could pull the trigger, if you felt your life was in danger, don't carry a gun, because it'll be just one more thing your attacker'll be able to use against you. But if he did follow you here from California, he's dangerous, even if he's never been violent. You need to be careful. Let me get you a receipt, and I'll call you tomorrow."

Chapter Two

When we'd arrived at six a.m. the neighborhood had been dark, the sky just starting to lighten. By six-thirty it was daylight and details had begun to emerge. The claimant's house was a two-story brick and wood edifice probably constructed during the Baby Boom. It seemed in decent shape, with some bright flowers out front. If she'd planted them, they might provide me an opportunity to get video of her doing a little gardening. Probably nothing that would violate her medical restrictions, but enough to justify my paycheck.

Only a third of the block was vacant lots covered in knee-high, unmown grass, and only one house on the block was boarded up which, for Detroit, made it an unremarkable residential area. Jerry was a hundred yards past her house on the opposite side of the street, hunkered down in the back seat of his Ford Explorer behind tinted windows.

Morning surveillances were usually very peaceful, if not downright boring. Watch the squirrels run around, listen to the birds chirp. With school out for the summer, there just wasn't a lot of early morning activity in the depths of the city neighborhoods. Only two cars on the entire block took off before nine a.m., their drivers presumably heading to work. As for what the rest of the residents of the neighborhood did for money, I could only guess.

Jerry's voice popped out of the handheld Motorola radio in the cupholder of my Tahoe. Loud. "Hey, did you hear about that Glove guy?" The radios would only reach half a mile in the city, but that was just fine for stationary surveillances, and most of the time while following someone. Beyond that distance we had cell phones.

I turned the volume down on the handheld. "The who?"

"The old guy we did surveillance on last fall. Domestic case, not insurance. Rich Detroit OG."

"Please don't try to sound like a gangster rapper, you're not P. Puff Diddy Daddy. Or is there a Snoop in there somewhere? Snoop Diggity?" I smiled behind the radio.

"Oh my God." He was almost choking. "Please stop. And you think I sound white? You know the case I mean. You and Mike did most of it, but I did one day, I think. Maybe two. He got killed in a carjacking. Him and his wife."

"Mitton," I told him.

"That's it. I was close. Just a little too slow getting out of the Bentley and gets popped by some crackhead idiot. Probably by accident, too, seeing as how it sounded from a witness like the dude panicked after the shooting and ran away without robbing him or the wife. Or taking the car." According to news reports the car had been paused at a stop sign when one man approached on foot. "How much was he worth, millions?"

"You can't take it with you."

"No, but it'd be nice to have while you're here. If I had the money for a Bentley, I wouldn't buy a Bentley. But then again I'm not an old dude or a rapper. Now his business gets it all, I guess. Shareholders or whoever. Seeing as we never could spot a girlfriend."

"Presumably."

We sat in silence for another ten minutes, staring at the nurse's house. Waiting for something to happen. Apparently she was in no hurry to run errands. The house began to shimmer slightly as the summer sun baked the concrete. I was parked in the shade of a maple with the engine off and all my windows cracked, but the humidity was awful. I'd be starting the car and blasting the A/C before long. And peeing in a bottle. The joys and romance of surveillance. I shifted in the seat, feeling my pistol poking me in the side. A full-size SIG P226 in a hip holster—hard to conceal, and not comfortable to sit on, but what it lacked in physical comfort it more than made up for in peace of mind.

"Hey, how long does that take?" Jerry said suddenly over the Motorola.

"How long does what take?"

"Getting your money after someone dies. Inheritance or whatever."

He was so young he had no experience with wills or settling estates. "That depends if there's a will or not. With a will it should be a lot quicker...theoretically. But the rich are different, and the more money there is, the more hassle. Someone always challenges the will, a black sheep son or daughter who's not getting a big enough slice of the pie, a bastard child or mistress who shows up at the last minute, a business partner arguing about stocks. Paternity, DNA tests, lawsuits, courtroom drama. If he didn't have a will, which I can't imagine, it'll go to probate, which takes forever. Either way, at a minimum, it will be months. More likely years, the lawyers bleeding the estate for two hundred bucks an hour. Apiece."

"He have kids?"

I thought back to the Freep article I'd skimmed. "I don't think so."

"I guess that's better, right?" I didn't respond, and a few seconds later he got back on the radio, his voice hollow. "Oh, shit, John, I…."

"Forget about it."

Other than poking her head out the front door to check to see if the mail had arrived, our nurse claimant didn't do a thing before we had eight hours on the clock. I told Jerry to meet me back there at eight the next morning, and headed into the office, arriving by two-thirty. I called Kerrie Edwards' cell phone a little before four p.m., and she got back with me within the hour.

"Well, the bad news is that his name is Michael Sullivan."

I could hear my client frowning on the other end of the line. "I don't understand."

"It's a common name, unlike Kerrie with an I-E."

"Did you run me?" She sounded surprised.

"No, just giving you an example. But, luckily, you had his Social Security number. That helps a lot, especially with credit card companies. I ran a comp report on him, non-criminal court records, talked to my contacts at a few utility and credit card companies…Unfortunately, or fortunately, I can find no evidence that he's in the state. None. If he's living here, his name is not on the lease or the mortgage. He's not paying any bills with checks or a credit card. If he's staying in a cheap hotel, or with a friend, hasn't gotten a job locally, and is paying cash for everything, he can stay under the radar. For weeks. Or months. But that won't last forever." A general search online for 'Michael Sullivan' had been totally useless except to remind me that it was the name of the character played by Tom Hanks the year before in the movie *Road to Perdition*.

"Darn it. I know it's him."

"Does he have any friends or relatives living in the area?"

"Not that I know of."

"I ran the plate on the Mustang. It's still registered to him in California. Doesn't expire for a couple of months." She'd been right, it was a 1988 Mustang, a GT, back from when they still had corners instead of curves. He didn't have any other vehicles registered to him, but if he was following her, and truly crazy or obsessed, I wouldn't have been surprised if he was using several different vehicles, and she only noticed the Mustang because it stuck out. She'd told me he was an auto mechanic. If he was working somewhere, maybe under the table for cash, he might have access to other vehicles.

"So what should I do now?"

"Do what I said. Head over to the Troy Police Department and file that information report. Then we can talk about what other steps we can take, surveillance or whatever."

"I'm just getting off work, so I'll drive straight over there. I've got to work tomorrow, and I hate to take another day off… How early do you get in the office?"

"If you want to stop by my office tonight after you're done at the PD, I'll be here," I told her. I had nowhere else to be.

I grabbed a sandwich at a nearby deli and then returned to my office to wait for Ms. Edwards. I didn't have a TV in the office, and I couldn't decide whether that was a mistake or a blessing. In various drawers and shelves of my office over the years I'd stashed books I knew I should read but had never gotten around to. A disintegrating marriage was giving me all sorts of free time I'd never had before. Currently I was about a third of the way through Hemingway's Islands In The Stream—I was reaching the end of 'Bimini', the first book of three inside the novel, when Kerrie Edwards knocked on the door. I waved her to the seat across the desk and put the book away, and shoved the remains of my dinner into the trash.

"Any problems at the PD?"

"No." She seemed in a better mood. "They said they'd have officers do some drive-bys of the house and keep a lookout for his car."

"Maybe they'll get lucky and he'll do something stupid, and they catch him in the act. But chances are you'll have one, maybe two cars a day drive by your house looking for his car. For maybe a week, before they move on to other pressing matters."

"So what can you do?" she asked me pointedly.

"Surveillance," I told her. "Sit on you and wait to see if he shows up. But you can invest a lot of time in a surveillance without anything to show for it. Meanwhile, you're paying me by the hour."

"How much?"

I told her, and she made a face.

"I'm worth it," I assured her with a smile. "But I don't want you to waste your money. You're pretty sure he knows where your mother lives, but he doesn't come to the house, you've only seen him while driving?"

"Right."

"Heading to work from home, to home from work, to school? You said you're working toward a CPA, right?"

"Yes, taking accounting classes at OCC. Night classes twice a week." She thought for a bit. "I know I've seen him twice on my way to work, two or three times on the way home. Maybe once at the college, at the far end of the parking lot, I'm not sure."

"Well, maybe it's all your imagination. Or somebody who lives in your mom's neighborhood has a car that looks like his. Hope springs eternal. But just in case...I think following you from home to work and back for a few days, also to school, would be the best bang for your buck. He's not coming to your home or workplace. If it is him, he's hanging back, and just following you in his car. From a distance. So I'll tail you, and see if I spot him. I've got a lot of experience doing that. And that way you're not paying me to sit for hours and hours when you're at work or sleeping."

"Okay, I guess." Her good mood after leaving the police department had evaporated. "How much would that cost?"

I'd punched her mother's address up on Mapquest. I practically had to drive past it to get from my current apartment accommodations to my office, and told her so. "You're barely out of my way. Pay me for four hours in advance, and that should cover a week of slight detours. I've got a full day surveillance scheduled tomorrow, but other than that I don't have anything else that should conflict." I was giving her a bargain because I felt sorry for her. Plus, if she wasn't crazy, and her ex had followed her from L.A. to Detroit, in violation of a restraining order, he could be real trouble. "Why don't you write out your schedule for me, and the address of your job." I looked at her and smiled. "And we can hope for the best. I sincerely hope you're wasting your money, but hope is not a strategy. You're doing the right thing. Do you have a better photo of him? That driver's license photo is pretty small."

She chewed at her lip. It would have been sexy if she hadn't obviously been so worried. "Yeah, I think so. I'll look for it when I get home."

Chapter Three

Kerrie Edwards lived with her mother in a two-story colonial with an attached two-car garage on Muer Drive, which ran east and west off Crooks Road in Troy. The street showed a mix of homes—older single-story ranches interspersed with boxier two-story homes, all on larger lots with mature trees. Middle-, maybe upper-middle-class income tax bracket.

Muer itself was a ribbon of blacktop, barely wide enough for two cars to pass. No sidewalks anywhere to be seen. It didn't seem like anybody parked on the street, which would make surveillance of the house difficult for Sullivan, if in fact he was stalking her. There was no sign of the Mustang on Muer or on either of the two residential streets which paralleled it.

I arrived early and drove past the house a few times. The garage door was closed, no vehicles visible, but a light was on inside. I took Muer west off Crooks, past the house, and found it dead-ended at Alpine Road a quarter-mile in.

Turning left on Alpine I took it south just over a half a mile, straight and flat as an arrow, where it exited directly onto Big Beaver. After I-75, Big Beaver was the largest and busiest street in the city, three lanes both east and west, lined by restaurants and business, the lanes separated by a large landscaped median.

Edwards had to head west for both her work and school, so whether she exited her neighborhood on Alpine or drove west on Muer and south on Crooks, she'd end up heading west on Big Beaver. At the intersection of Alpine and Big Beaver were a McDonald's to one side and a strip mall struggling to look upscale on the other. Someone wanting to follow a resident could sit in one of those lots and just wait for the car to drive by on Big Beaver. Or down Alpine, where it would pause at the stop sign. Ms. Edwards drove a little white Toyota which would be easy enough to spot, if you knew to look for it. I drove around the McDonald's and all through the large parking lot of the strip mall, but there was no sign of the Mustang.

Between people arriving early for work and the drive-through traffic there was a decent amount of vehicular traffic in the area. I spotted a number of people sitting in cars—too many for me to eyeball each and every one to see if the driver matched the photo I had of Sullivan. I called Jerry a little after seven.

"Am I late? I thought we were starting at eight."

"We are. You are. I'm working something else. I might be a little late. So don't you be."

"Roger that."

Then I called my claimant. "You normally leave about seven-forty?"

"Usually. Unless I'm running late. It only takes me about ten minutes to get to work."

"What route do you usually take?"

"I turn left out of the driveway and go down the street until it dead ends. I don't know the name of that street, but I turn left and take that down to Big Beaver. I take that to Woodward. It's the quickest way."

"Okay. Just head to work the way you normally do. Don't look for me. There's no sign of him in the area, but like you said, you never see him at the house."

"O-Okay."

Despite what I'd said, when she pulled up to the stop sign in her little car I could see her craning her neck around, looking for me. She pulled out into a break in traffic. I was in the McDonald's parking lot and waited about ten seconds. No one drove down Alpine behind her, and no car pulled out of either nearby parking lot after she made the turn.

I pulled out of the McDonald's lot directly onto Big Beaver, cutting someone off, and sped up to keep her car in sight. I stayed only as close as I needed to make it through the same traffic lights, and tried to avoid being in the same lane. The experience was a bit unusual for me—normally I've only got eyes for the person I'm following. Following Edwards I had to force my eyes off her car and scan all the others.

Minivans were the quintessential surveillance vehicle but I'd never been a fan of them. They just weren't good in snow, and Michigan generally had six months of winter. Plus, they had small car tires. Several times a week I found the need to hop a curb or a parking stone and if you try that in a minivan you'll tear out your undercarriage. I much preferred SUVs and always equipped them with all-terrain tires.

The Tahoe was a little big, but it didn't really stick out,

whether parked or moving in traffic. That was the most important thing to successfully following people without being spotted. Well, there were two big things. Number one was having a vehicle that didn't stick out—sorry, as much as I love Magnum P.I. and Tom Selleck, nobody could follow someone in a red Ferrari without getting spotted. You need a common vehicle in a drab color. My Tahoe has a boring Chevy bowtie on the grille, and is black. Number two is, if at all possible, don't do anything that draws attention to yourself or your vehicle.

I liked that the Tahoe was big enough I could easily crawl over the seats into the back and film out any window. It had dark limo tint all around. With the way sunlight bounced off windshield, as long as I wasn't wearing brightly-colored clothing or moving around, even sitting in the front seat I was barely visible to anyone looking through the windshield because of all the black behind me. I just wasn't silhouetted.

I also liked the Tahoe's size for another reason; I'd been chased and blocked in by angry claimants on a number of occasions, long before I was targeted by serious government types. Bigger cars have more mass, which means a better chance of success if I ever needed to ram other vehicles to get out of a situation.

After three miles on Big Beaver, Edwards turned north onto Woodward Avenue, and as soon as she did I dropped way back, driving as slowly as I could in the right lane to put some distance between us, looking to see if anybody passed me to stick close to her. Not quite a mile up was a two-story office building on the right, and she was just barely in my sight as she pulled into the lot. I took the loop-around on Woodward, which had its own grassy median, waited for a break in traffic while watching her building in my mirrors, and pulled into the lot of the office building on the far side. I sat and watched the two driveways to her workplace.

Ten minutes later my phone rang, just before I was about to call her. "Were you there? I didn't see you."

"That's the point. So he doesn't see me either. I didn't see any sign of his Mustang, and nobody pulled into the lot right after you."

"You probably think I'm crazy, that I'm just imagining this. Him."

"A restraining order is pretty damn real. And better safe than sorry. You're off at four-thirty?"

"Yeah. But I've got class tonight, at six, so instead of heading home and just turning right around I usually just drive straight up there."

"I should be back here by four-thirty. I'll give you a call."

"Okay." She didn't sound happy. There was no reason for her to be.

I rolled into the nurse claimant's neighborhood right at eight-thirty and parked in my usual spot. Jerry's vehicle was just visible at the far end of the street. I grabbed the Motorola. "I miss anything?"

"I rolled in at seven fifty-eight," he told me flatly. "Her car was already gone."

"Goddammit." I sighed. "Well, let's sit on it. Adjuster gets in at nine, and I'll give her a call, see if she wants us to break it off, sit on it, do a knock, whatever."

At nine twenty-three I called Jerry on the radio. "Just got off the phone with Michelle. Apparently the claimant is back to work with the insured. Nobody thought to tell her."

"Well, that's a couple hours on the paycheck that I wouldn't have gotten otherwise," he said, always the optimist. "Although the rest of the day is shot."

"You available this afternoon?" I asked him. "Say from four to six? Maybe more, depending." I wouldn't mind a second set of eyes looking for Sullivan. And I'd already come to the realization that I'd probably be putting in far more hours on Ms. Edwards' behalf than she'd paid for. Than she could afford to pay for.

"Sure. Whaddaya got?"

"A stalker thing. Meet me at four at the southwest corner of Lone Pine and Woodward. I think that's Birmingham. Office building parking lot. I'll give you the particulars. And I've got two or three more work comp surveillance cases for the rest of this week and next, I just have to figure out what needs to be done when."

"No worries."

Ten minutes after Kerrie Edwards headed into the building for her accounting class Jerry and I were parked door-to-door in the parking lot.

"I'm guessing she doesn't have back or knee problems," he said drily. "But a stalker, I get. You sure you don't need me to get video?"

"Yeah." Although Jerry's longtime girlfriend, Jodi, made Kerrie Edwards look ugly. 'Slim and stacked' I believe was an appropriately descriptive phrase, and Jodi had a pretty face in addition to the curves.

"You think he's really been following her?" We'd seen no sign of Sullivan or the Mustang following her from her workplace to the school. She attended classes at the big Orchard Ridge Campus in Farmington Hills. Lone Pine to

Splits and Transitions

Telegraph to I-696 to Orchard Lake Road—over ten miles to spot anyone tailing her.

I shrugged. "We've both seen crazier things."

"Yeah, no shit." He looked around. "We done here? Or are we putting her to bed?"

"Go ahead and take off. Start that new case tomorrow at six. Don't forget to call in to the PD, though, Clarkston isn't Detroit. The neighbors call in on a strange car on the street and you'll have two cruisers on you in no time, red and blues lighting up the whole block. They've got nothing else to do." We never had problems doing surveillances in Detroit, Flint, Saginaw, etc. Cops there were too busy dealing with actual crime. If we forgot to call into the department and notify them of our presence ahead of time it was the suburbs where we got hassled by bored officers hoping we were up to no good.

"Will do."

I grabbed my sunglasses off the dash and he saw my hand shaking. "You okay?"

"I hit the gym hard this afternoon. Shoulders and chest. I can barely lift my arms."

"You're getting big. You working out a lot?"

I'd put on at least ten pounds of muscle in the past three months. "Every day. Stress release with the divorce and…all that." He gave me a look, like he was my dad. "Hey, better working out than drinking," I told him. "I'll be running this one in the morning, so call me if you've got any issues. And Mike's doing a surveillance in Lake Orion starting at nine, so you guys will be relatively close to each other if things get squirrelly and you need another body. Or he does."

He started his car and took off with a wave and chirp of his tires.

I grabbed my shifter and was about to put my Tahoe in

gear, then paused, and instead shut my engine off. I could see her car from where I was sitting. I might as well follow her home and hang around a bit, just in case. I had nothing else to do.

Chapter Four

Three days later I was driving to the office from the gym after working out for lunch. My thighs were quivering, on the verge of cramping up, which perhaps wasn't such a great idea considering how much traffic there was on the road. I managed to catch the top-of-the-hour news break on WJR.

"Today, some surprising developments in the death of Detroit icon Bernard Mitton. The successful businessman and one-time member of the Detroit City Council died last week in an attempted carjacking, shot dead beside his wife. Today, the lawyer for his estate made Mitton's will public, and it seems he left the majority of his millions not to his wife but to another woman, Esther Parnell, who is reported to be his long-time mistress."

"Son of a bitch, she was right," I swore. He had been having an affair. And had been able to successfully hide it from me and my guys, at least for the week we'd been following him. We hadn't spotted the girlfriend...and if Michael Sullivan was following Kerrie Edwards, I hadn't been able to spot him either. Apparently I wasn't as good as I thought I was.

Two minutes later my phone rang. It was Jerry Phillips. "Did you catch the news?" He was on surveillance, which usually meant his radio was on and turned to talk radio.

"About Mitton?"

"Yeah. Was he too slick for us? Or did he just not happen to hook up with her while we were following him around?"

"My ego is requesting I choose the latter option."

"Yeah. Hey, what are you doing tonight?"

"Taking Kerrie Edwards from work back to her house, looking for our invisible man. After that…." Probably heading home and watching TV. Maybe working out again to blow off some anger, I could have told him, but didn't.

"George Kelly's in town. We're invited for dinner."

At George's name my heart thudded in my chest and I had to physically calm myself down. While I'd spoken to him on the phone several times since, the last time I'd actually seen the man was December. In Maryland. At a roadblock. While I was being roughly handcuffed in spite of my broken arm. And broken foot. And concussion, from the grenade. Grenades. And I'd been in better shape than half of us. Traditional PI work like following someone through Detroit in rush hour traffic seemed positively tranquil in comparison.

"What time?"

"Six. But get there when you can get there."

"Right." My phone beeped and I looked at it. "I've got another call."

"See you later."

It was Mike, the retired cop who worked for me nearly

full-time to supplement his pension. "I'm pretty sure it counts as abuse," he said.

"What?"

"Having to deal with government employees."

I smiled into my phone. I'd sent him down to the City-County Building in Detroit and then up to the Oakland County Courthouse in Pontiac to get copies of a number of different cases. I hated doing it. Not because of the often-surly public employees, but rather because of the metal detectors. I didn't like to take my gun off anywhere at any time for any reason.

It's not paranoia when people have tried to kill you. Repeatedly.

Jerry was of the same mind. He'd accompanied me on that famous cross-country adventure the year before, along with a number of our mutual friends, and we'd all almost died about twenty times. Mike, on the other hand, was like a lot of former cops—he didn't carry a gun, not even when doing surveillance. Hadn't carried one off-duty when he'd still been on the job. I didn't understand cops like that, but I knew they were out there. And I didn't try to change him, I'd been around long enough to know that attempting to change people never worked.

"Think of it as a way to build character, or practice patience with your fellow humans," I told him. He just grunted into the phone. "Did you find what we were looking for?" A single-shingle lawyer used us as his investigators from time to time, and he'd needed us to get copies of an old divorce and some civil lawsuits that related to a client he'd just taken on.

"Yeah. It took forever, but I got them. The computers they use there are older than the space program."

"You still up in Pontiac?"

"You told me to call you while I was still up here," he reminded me.

"Good. Head on down Telegraph to Robinson's office in Southfield and pick up a couple of subpoenas he's got for us to deliver. That's kind of on your way home. Then you can either bring them by later today or tomorrow, whatever is easiest for you. Or serve them yourself if they're nearby, I don't know where they're going."

"I'll look them over and let you know. It might depend on how bad traffic is," he told me. "But I'll need to get you these copies."

"And don't forget to expense them."

"With what they charge per page? I won't, don't worry."

I'd been sitting at my desk for half an hour, thinking, before finally looking up a number and dialing the phone. Not being able to spot Kerrie Edwards' stalker had been bothering me, and the news about Mitton's girlfriend, mistress, whoever, had me doubting myself.

"World's Greatest Detective," I heard in my ear.

"Isn't that Sherlock Holmes?"

"World's Greatest *Living* Detective," he corrected himself. "How's Detroit?"

"Decomposing. How's L.A.?"

"Sunny, beautifully deranged, and in love with itself. I wouldn't have it any other way. What's up?"

"I've got a case, young lady moved here from there, in large part to avoid a stalker. But…" I made a face and shook my head. "I've got a feeling that I'm missing something. That there's something else going on. Haven't seen any sign of him out here since I've been looking, but she's convinced she's spotted him."

"Unless she's crazy. Or making the whole thing up."

"The thought has crossed my mind. But she got a

restraining order against him in L.A. before moving out here."

"Have you seen this restraining order?"

"No."

"Would you like to?"

I smiled. "That's why I'm calling. And anything else pertinent or interesting you can pull up on either one of them while you're down at the courthouse flirting with the ladies. I can fax you all the particulars."

"I'm on it."

George Kelly lived on Silverbell Road about half a mile east of Adams, officially a mile north of Rochester Hills proper in Oakland Township. Twenty years earlier the area had been farms and fields, but the subdivisions had spread northward from Rochester Hills like a fungus and were filling in every available space.

Kelly's house was a sprawling ranch on perhaps ten acres, with a large detached barn to one side. The first time I'd visited there had been nothing but fields stretching in every direction, but now a subdivision nearly filled with McMansions bordered his property to the west, and a golf course was under construction to the north. Silverbell itself, which had been gravel forever, had just been paved over with asphalt.

Progress.

Rochester Hills, and Oakland Township, were upper middle class, and the subdivisions were filled with three-to-five-thousand square foot luxury homes with three-car garages on small lots. The mile-long stretch of Adams Road between Dutton Road to the south and Silverbell to the north was known as the "Billion Dollar Mile" for the total value of the properties on either side. If he ever decided to sell Kelly was sitting on a goldmine with his acreage. Of course, the developer would just tear down the house and barn and put in a short street filled with big houses perched right atop one another.

From the number of cars in the driveway it appeared I was one of the last to arrive. I parked around the side and went in through the garage. The back hall led directly to the kitchen, where I found George Kelly laboring over something. Physically he was a freak of nature—less than six feet tall, but improbably thick everywhere. With not much fat on his body he was probably pushing three hundred pounds, built like an oil drum set on two stumps. He'd once told me it was family genetics—back during the Depression his first-generation immigrant Irish great-uncle had worked as a cop in Chicago, and the man had been six-eight, which for that era was a monster. Kelly's son, Ron, had huge calves, but otherwise was physically unremarkable.

"There's beer in the fridge," George said to me without turning around.

I smiled and retrieved one, dancing out of his way as he moved quickly about the kitchen. "How you doin', George?" He looked good. He'd maybe lost a bit of weight, and had a tan. Not surprising, considering where he'd been spending most of his time.

"Tired." He paused. "Glad to be home."

"How long you back for?"

He shrugged.

"Don't know, or can't tell me?" He did work for the CIA, after all, and we were in the middle of a global war on terror. In January I'd been told he was in Syria. Since then we could only guess, although he was able to call home once or twice a week.

Splits and Transitions

I caught the edge of a smile on his face. "Don't know, actually. I'm not supposed to be a field guy. Not any more. Hell, I'm supposed to be semi-retired. But…you know." He shrugged. "Lot of people need killing. And I know a few things."

"Yeah." We'd invaded Iraq three months earlier. Everyone in the military and intelligence services seemed to be working twenty-five-hour days.

"Home a couple weeks, I'm hoping. Long enough for the wife to be happy when I leave. Unless I decide to pull the pin for good. This is a young man's game, and I'm a lot older than I used to be."

He was chopping a lot of vegetables, but it wasn't for a salad. I saw beef cut into strips, rolled in some sort of seasoning. "Fajitas?" I guessed.

"That's the plan."

Several people were sitting around the table in the dining area—Jerry Phillips, Ron Kelly, and Steve Reath. The whole crew apart from Bob Grinnand, who was still recovering after having died—briefly, but it didn't take—on our cross-country misadventure in December. I wandered over. "Gentlemen," I said with a nod, taking a swig of beer.

Jerry and Steve had just graduated from college. Ron had changed his major and was taking a number of science courses over the summer toward a forensics degree, although he still had at least another year of school. Not one of them was twenty-three years old yet, but despite our age difference we were as close as men got.

"How you doing?" Steve asked me.

I looked back and forth between their faces, and figured out they'd been talking about me. I opened my mouth to tell them to mind their own business, or maybe make a smartass comment, but instead I just made a face and drank some more beer. They nodded.

"Somebody get the door," George called out. He had a big plate of raw meat in his hands. Ron jumped up and pulled open the sliding patio door, and we found ourselves outside around the grill as George cooked the meat. The June evening was cool and pleasant, the humidity only a little too high for comfort, which for summer in Michigan was as good as it got.

"I already heard back from the DEA," Steve told us. He hadn't been able to apply to be a Special Agent with the DEA—a job I'd had in a past life—until he'd graduated from MSU. Which had been less than two months earlier. "I'm scheduled for a physical and drug test in three weeks."

"Seriously?" Jerry said. He looked from Steve to me. "What the hell? Marshals Service hasn't done jack yet."

I shrugged. "All of the feds are getting increased tax dollars to help out with the war on terror, but the DEA already works all over the world with foreign governments. They're in a better position to help, so they're probably getting more money. Which means they're probably short on bodies, and hiring as fast as they can. Marshals, on the other hand, is all domestic and doesn't deal with terrorists or drugs."

"What about the Air Marshals?" Ron asked. "That's terrorism."

"That's DHS, not U.S. Marshals," I told him. I looked back at Jerry. "You could apply to the FBI."

"Not until I'm twenty-three," he said with some exasperation. Which was most of a year away.

"There's always the military," George told him. He'd been an Army MP before joining the CIA.

"Yeah, I know. But I want to use my brain. And the degree I just spent four years getting."

George just shrugged. There was no question about bravery, self-sacrifice, or service to country on the part of anyone there. George had been kidnapped by a traitorous co-worker, and to rescue him we'd left a trail of bodies from Michigan to Maryland, in the process recovering intelligence that saved lives. Hundreds of thousands of lives, if not more. Still, if it wasn't for "national security" we'd all be in prison. Sixty-one people dead by our hands. And we couldn't talk to anyone about it except each other, every single bit of what had happened was now classified Top Secret and compartmentalized. Not that anyone would believe us even if we'd started talking.

I'd been tortured. Bob Grinnand, their high school friend who was now a Sergeant in the Army Special Forces, a Green Beret, had been shot multiple times. His fiancée had been killed by a bomb meant for him. Jerry'd been shot through the chest and suffered cracked ribs and a collapsed lung, perhaps the most serious wounds of any of us had suffered apart from Bob. I glanced at Ron's ear, which had been split in half by a bullet. After one more cosmetic surgery it now looked more like an ear than not, but it would never be pretty. I knew, without having to look, they were all carrying guns. Probably legally, for once, now that they were over twenty-one and Michigan had become a 'shall issue' state for concealed weapons permits. We'd all recovered physically, but we were still experiencing more than a bit of PTSD. And we'd earned it.

"And the DEA doesn't care that I tried weed a couple times?" Steve asked me. He nervously fingered the gap on his left hand where his ring finger should have been, shot off after we'd found George but before we'd managed to escape—right into the hands of the police, who'd assumed we were terrorists. They weren't completely wrong.

"To be honest, if you told them you'd never tried marijuana they wouldn't believe you. Not these days. So, no."

"I know I'm going to pass the drug test, and the physical. After that…there's the polygraph." We all exchanged a look.

"Just say what we were told to say."

"Have you ever committed a crime, Mr. Reath?" Jerry asked him in an officious voice, I suppose doing his best imitation of a polygraph examiner.

Steve looked at him, and doing his best to sound just as officious replied, "I'm sorry, Sir, I can't answer that question. You will need to speak to the Director of the FBI's Counterintelligence Division." He looked at me and rolled his eyes. "You really think that's going to fly?"

"It's all you can do. They'll give you grief, of course. Assume you're full of shit. But you're going to be hooked to a polygraph. Ask them, 'When I told you I couldn't answer that question and said you needed to speak to the Director of the FBI's Counterintelligence Division…was I lying?'"

"Christ."

"Lemme know how that goes," Jerry said, drinking more beer. "Marshals don't poly, but you never know." He looked at me. "Don't we have a phone number of someone we can call?"

"That's for emergencies related to the content of the Department of State non-disclosure agreements we all signed. If new information pops up, or the few people involved who aren't dead or in jail decide to come after us. It's not to smooth out pre-employment polygraphs."

"Federal government pre-employment polygraphs with questions you can't, by law, answer, seem like something that would be directly related to the content of the NDAs you signed," George said from behind the grill. He shrugged his huge shoulders. "It couldn't hurt to make a call." We exchanged a look. He did have a point.

"So how are you doing?" Ron asked me. They all knew about the in-progress divorce. And the reasons behind it.

"Awesome. Fucking great." I drank the rest of my beer and went inside to get another one, hoping they'd drop the subject. But when I came back out they were all looking at me.

"Sure you're okay?" Steve asked me.

"Stop fucking asking me that."

In part, I was working out all the time in the hope I'd be so tired that I wouldn't dream. Still, at least half the time I had nightmares. The accusing faces of the people I'd killed. That we'd all killed.

Sixty-one dead. Not counting my dog, or the baby growing inside my wife.

My son.

Chapter Five

"I think my husband is cheating on me," I heard in my ear. "Well, I know he's cheating on me, but I have to…know. Do you do that? Follow people? Cheating husbands, or…oh God, that sounds so tawdry. Like I'm in a soap opera." I heard her fight back a sob.

"Yes ma'am, I do that kind of work," I said soothingly. I'd had this same conversation with potential clients a number of times.

"Do you do a lot of it?"

"I do what comes my way. It's not exactly predictable. Or steady. Insurance fraud and work comp claims pay most of the bills, the only things sure in this life are death, taxes, and insurance." I almost added adultery, but stopped myself. "But yes, I've done quite a bit of these kind of…your kind of cases. Cheating husband, wife, boyfriend, girlfriend, you name it."

Normally, by the time somebody works up the nerve to call a private investigator, there is not a doubt in their mind that their spouse or significant other is cheating on them.

Splits and Transitions

PIs aren't cheap, but more importantly hiring someone to investigate someone you love, or at least used to, is a huge step. We get hired for peace of mind, so they can prove to themselves that they aren't crazy. Michigan is a no-fault divorce state, so proof of infidelity has no bearing on the divorce proceedings.

Technically.

That said, if you can document the other half in your relationship was stepping out on you, it is great leverage in getting more alimony, or custody time with the kids, or whatever it is you're angling for in the divorce proceedings. Even in our modern era, shame is a powerful motivator, and if you threaten to show pictures—or better yet, video—of your spouse meeting someone at a restaurant or hotel, stealing kisses, or even steaming up the windows of a car, when that video might be seen by their children or parents...

"So, how do I—how do we do this? How do I hire you? And what would you do?"

I leaned back in my chair. "Generally what works is surveillance, but why don't you tell me the situation, and I'll give you my recommendations. Let's start with names. I'm John."

She sighed in my ear, and I heard a hiccup. She was still fighting back tears. "Melinda. Melinda Kern. We've been drifting apart for years. We've been married for over twenty years. We haven't...well, we're just not intimate. Not really. Small talk. That's it. And for the past few months, every Friday, he doesn't come home from work. Not until two, maybe three in the morning."

"What does he say he's been doing?"

"Going to bars. *Unwinding.* And he does smell like alcohol when he comes home, comes to bed. I'm always awake, but I've started pretending to be asleep. Otherwise we fight. And I cry. And I hate crying. But I know it's not that. Not just that. He's not just out drinking. There's something else going on."

"Doing surveillance on him, on a Friday, to see where he's going, seems like the best play then."

"Okay. So how do I hire you?"

"I've got a short, one page client contract I'll need you to sign. Then I'm hired. Well, and payment, of course. Something like this, I'll need a deposit up front. This surveillance would have a pretty narrow focus, so I don't see me burning up a lot of hours on it. Say five hundred dollars. Cash or check, although if you pay by check I wait for it to clear before starting work." On domestic cases I always took my payment up front. I'd learned that the hard way. Sometimes they didn't have the money to afford me to begin with...or when I didn't find evidence of cheating, they refused to pay. Or when I did get video of the wife or husband with someone on the side, my client would get so angry they'd refuse to pay. Bearer of bad tidings, etc. Generally I preferred working for faceless insurance companies and dealing with adjusters who had no personal interest in my results, or animus toward anyone involved, but I wasn't wealthy enough to turn down clients. And this case sounded easy enough. "Would you like to come in to the office? Or can I fax you a copy of the contract?"

"Oh God no. I'll come in. If I'm wrong...I can't have him knowing. What I did. But I'm not wrong."

Which was how I found myself in a small industrial park in Livonia late on a Friday afternoon.

For all the headaches associated with domestic cases, they were easier to work in a lot of ways—the client provided a current photo, vehicle information with license plate, work schedule, everything they had. Information provided by insurance adjusters, on the other hand, was often incomplete, out of date, or just plain wrong.

William Kern was fifty-six years old and didn't work for anyone, he owned his own small business, with twenty-two employees. The building was on a short street that ran off the eastbound I-96 service drive halfway between Middlebelt and Merriman Roads. He drove a two-year-old Cadillac STS which was parked in front of the long one-story building when I rolled up at four-thirty in the afternoon. Technically the business was only open until five p.m., which definitely had me wondering what Mr. Kern was doing until two or three in the morning.

Mike was already there, his mini-van parked in a nearby parking lot between the subject's business and the service drive. I moved farther into the industrial park, in another parking lot, and took the long eye. I was farther away, but had a better angle on Kern's car and the front of his business, The KBR Group. The parking lot was between it and the adjoining building, and mostly out of sight.

Employees began trickling out of the building by ones and twos a little after five. At five forty-five, I hadn't seen anyone leave the building for quite some time. "Mike," I said into the Motorola, "do a drive-by. How many cars are left in the lot?"

"Hold on."

Thirty seconds later I saw his mini-van drive by the front of the building. "None. Just his," I heard. "I'm going to loop around, so he doesn't see me twice. Back into the same spot, seems to be working for me."

"Roger that."

Just before six-thirty a figure exited the front door of KBR and headed for the Cadillac. I raised the binoculars. It was Kern. He was slender and had evenly graying hair cut short, wearing khakis and a blue button-down shirt. "He's out," I keyed into the radio.

But instead of opening the driver door of his car, he popped the trunk. He bent down into it, retrieved an object, closed the trunk, and headed back inside.

"He's back inside," I told Mike over the radio. "He grabbed something out of the trunk." I paused, then said slowly, "I think it was a bottle of wine." He'd been too far away to be sure. "His car's the only one in the lot?"

"Yeah. Maybe the party's coming to him. I'll keep an eye out for anyone turning into the lot."

We were only a week out from the longest day of the year, and it stayed light until after nine o'clock. Mike continued doing drive-bys of the building every hour or so, but reported no other cars had snuck into the lot. The few windows in the front of the building had pebbled glass, so there was nothing to see from the outside.

Once it got dark I moved in closer, but still barely spotted Kern before he had the door of his car open and the inside light came on. "He's out!" I called into the radio.

"Fucking finally," Mike grumbled.

I glanced at the digital clock on my dashboard. 9:47.

Kern backed his Cadillac out onto the street, then headed toward the service drive. He turned right, heading eastbound, and by the time he did Mike was in front of him. It was a solid move by Mike—the service drive was one-way, so once we saw him heading that way, we knew which direction he would turn.

I was less than a quarter mile behind them when I turned onto the service drive. Most of the cars had their headlights on, but it wasn't quite dark enough to need them to see, they acted more like identifiers in the purple dusk.

Splits and Transitions

Up ahead I saw Mike's mini-van in the right lane, and Kern's Cadillac in the left beside it. I eyed the light ahead at Middlebelt and saw it was red, so I kept to the speed limit.

When I was a hundred yards back the light turned green. Kern accelerated quickly and moved to the left to jump on the on-ramp to eastbound I-96, then his Caddy disappeared from sight as it took the ramp down. I-96 through Livonia was forty feet below ground level, and at least four lanes in each direction, heading straight into downtown Detroit. Mike's van drifted over at the last minute and got on the on-ramp, and I moved in behind him.

"Shit!" I swore. Kern must have floored it as soon as he'd gotten on the ramp, his Cadillac was now far ahead of us. Mike saw the same thing as I did, and stomped on his accelerator, but his aging mini-van didn't exactly have a lot of horsepower.

Kern was out of sight around a curve up ahead. As soon as we reached the end of the ramp I floored the Tahoe and roared around Mike. A mile up I'd just caught sight of Kern's Cadillac, which had to be doing in excess of eighty miles an hour, when a construction zone closed off the two left lanes, and traffic stacked up in front of me. I couldn't get past them, there weren't any gaps. Kern, on the other hand, had open road in front of him, and I watched him disappear.

"Where is he? Where'd he go?" Mike said over the radio. I saw him appear in my rearview.

"Up past these ass-draggers. If I can find a gap maybe I can catch him."

A gap didn't open up for over a minute, and then I got honked at twice as I slalomed the Tahoe around slower moving cars in the construction zone. I got the SUV up to

110 once the orange barrels ended, but I never caught up to Kern's Cadillac. Whether he had too much of a lead on me, or had turned off somewhere, there was no way to know.

"He wasn't on to us, we'd barely been behind him when he took off," Mike said. "What's that STS have, three hundred horse? He hammered it." I didn't bother to respond, I was too pissed. "Wife give you any regular hangouts in Detroit?" Mike asked me.

"No. She doesn't know where he's going. That's why she hired me. Shit." Maybe I should give up PI work and become an accountant. My total inability to follow people wouldn't be an issue if I was an accountant.

"We going to be back here next Friday?"

"Yeah." I sighed. "Let's go back and sit on the business for fifteen minutes, just in case he only went out for smokes or whatever."

"You wish."

Chapter Six

I had today's copy of the Detroit News on the passenger seat as I waited in the parking lot of the McDonald's for Kerrie Edwards to leave for work. It and the Detroit Free Press were the two main papers in town, but ironically after a huge strike a few years back they had combined their business operations. Theoretically they still maintained separate editorial staffs. Technically and historically the News was the more conservative paper, and the Freep the liberal one, but seeing as they were both left of center and filled their news stories with editorialized opinions it was a distinction without a practical difference other than the title atop the front page. Which was probably why their circulations kept dropping.

What kept drawing my eye wasn't their politics, but rather a photo on the front page below the fold. Esther Parnell, standing just behind her attorney. For such an old-fashioned name, Bernard Mitton's mistress looked quite good. While she'd donned black for the occasion of her lawyer reading her statement to the press—she and Bernie adored each other, he was in a loveless marriage, they'd been together for years and he planned to leave his wife, if only she'd been able to bear him a child—she looked younger than her reported forty-two years of age. Slender, with red hair. Mitton's wife—his second—had been forty-nine, and she'd looked good as well sitting in my office chair. She was a blonde, and had some serious front-end work done, something that set her apart from the relatively flat-chested Ms. Parnell. Apparently, just because you bought something didn't mean you got to play with it. Still, there was a similarity in the facial features between the two women. I guess Mitton had a type.

He'd been a member of the Detroit City Council for a brief time back in the seventies where he was famous for his shouting arguments with Mayor Coleman Young. Young ended up being Mayor for twenty years, presiding over the slow-motion collapse of the city while Mitton made his millions. Mitton was a Korean War vet, I'd learned from the obit. I hadn't known that. One of the Chosin Few, which made him a true hero. And now he was dead in a pointless, random crime.

Ms. Edwards' Toyota rolled by me, stopped at the corner, and then pulled out onto Big Beaver. I looked around, waited ten seconds, didn't see anybody pull out into Monday morning rush hour to chase her, then followed her myself. I'd made the trip enough times that I was starting to get a feel for the traffic and adjust automatically, which allowed me to pay more attention to the people in the cars around us. Still no sign of her stalker.

She drove into the lot of her office building and I rolled through it behind her, just to check the cars. Nothing. Then

I pulled across Woodward into my usual spot. I'd barely parked before my phone rang.

"Anything?"

"Nope."

"I swear to God I'm not crazy," Kerrie Edwards said defensively into my ear.

"I never said you were," I said soothingly. While both Jerry and Mike had helped out a few times, I'd done most of the work on her. I'd used up all of her retainer, and then some. With zero results.

"No, but you're thinking it," she said.

I opened my mouth to respond, then saw the bright blue Mustang pull into the driveway of her office building and disappear behind it. "I've got a blue Mustang," I told her quickly. "Just pulled into your lot. Can you get to a window and look for it?"

"What? Yeah, hold on. Is it an old one?" I could hear her breathing as she walked.

"Eighties. In perfect shape. Electric blue, like you said."

"That sounds like his." There was a pause. "I can't see it. But I can only see half the lot from here."

"All right. I'm going to drive over and check it out. If it's him, and he actually comes up to see you before I get over there, you call me."

"Um...okay."

I pulled out onto Woodward and was waiting to do the loop-around when the Mustang nosed out of the far driveway, then pulled out, heading north on Woodward. It had tinted windows, but I could see there was a male in the car, alone. The vehicle had a Michigan license plate, although it was too far away to read. I was blocked by traffic and couldn't pull out immediately. When I was able to force myself past the idling cars the light in front of me was red, and the Mustang was already out of sight up Woodward. I checked the traffic to the left, then drove through the red light, and floored it. I'd barely made it a hundred yards before I spotted the red and blue lights behind me. And heard the whoop of the siren.

"Oh for fuck's sake, are you kidding me?"

I had a slim, vain hope that the cruiser was heading to a call unrelated to my traffic malfeasance, but no. I pulled into a parking lot off Woodward and by the time the Bloomfield Hills officer walked up to my door my window was down and my hands were on the steering wheel. My driver's license and Michigan CPL—concealed pistol license—were in my left hand.

"You didn't see me, sitting right there?" the cop said incredulously.

"Private investigator," I told him, sighing. "Trying to follow somebody, which apparently I've forgotten how to do. I'm armed," I told him, wiggling the CPL. He took the licenses while keeping an eye on me. Michigan law required we immediately notify any law enforcement officer we came in contact with that we were armed.

"Where is it?"

"Right hip." I had an authentic Colt AR-15 underneath the back seat, perfectly legal, and a loaded Wilson Combat shotgun all the way in the back, but he didn't need to know about those. Or the seven-inch Ka-Bar knife in the center console. Or that I had enough ammo in the Chevy to fight my way to Cleveland if necessary.

"Roger that, just keep it there. Who were you following?"

"Bright blue Mustang, older, popped into a lot right there at Lone Pine. Then took off north."

"What kind of case?"

"Stalker. If it was him. Was trying to catch up to find out."

"I saw that car. I was pulling out to chase after him for illegal tint on the windows when you tore ass past me."

I shook my head, then slowly leaned forward and banged it on the steering wheel a few times. Then I leaned back and sighed again.

"You ever on the job?" he asked me. A lot of private investigators got their start as cops.

"DEA," I told him. "In my youth. Detroit and Miami."

"Hang here," he told me, and headed back to his car. To run my name and DL. And probably write me a ticket, the way my week had been going. My cell phone rang.

"Was it him?" Kerrie sounded breathless.

"I don't know. The car had Michigan plates, but that doesn't mean anything. One guy inside. Tinted windows." I glanced in my rearview mirror at the spinning lights. "I was trying to chase it down, get close enough to read the plate, but…I got pulled over for speeding. Currently getting a ticket, probably. Just down Woodward."

"Seriously? I thought private investigators were allowed to do that kind of stuff."

"Wouldn't that be nice."

"So do you think it was him?"

"It was exactly the car you described. Pulling into your office parking lot early on a Monday morning, then pulling out less than a minute later. Which isn't time enough to do anything but drop somebody off. So…probably." I glanced up at the mirror and saw the cop was heading back my way. "I've gotta go. I'll call you later."

"I'm going to let you off with a warning," he told me, handing back my credentials.

"I appreciate it," I told him. I dug out a card and wrote on the back while I talked. "Look, the case I'm working, the young lady works in that office building right there on the corner. She got a restraining order against a guy who wouldn't take no for an answer. And he still wouldn't, so she moved here from California. It sure looks like he followed her, too, if that was his car. Which makes it serious."

"She get a PPO?"

"Hasn't been able to prove he's even in the state. That's what I'm supposed to be doing. So far, nothing. Until today. She lives in Troy, and filed a report with them, but she works in your town. If you can keep an eye out for that 'Stang, that California restraining order is still in effect. Would at least give you a reason to pull him over and talk to him." I shrugged and handed him my card, with Sullivan's name and car info on the back. "Might be more interesting than pulling over idiots who blow through red lights right in front of you."

He read the info on the back of the card. "That it might." He nodded and saluted me with the card as he headed back to his cruiser.

I'd been back at my office for an hour, nursing my wounds, when the phone rang. It was the World's Greatest Detective, via L.A.

"Sooooo. Ms. Edwards. Ms. Kerrie Edwards," he said in my ear. He seemed in a playful mood. "What's she like? Pretty?"

I wasn't sure where he was going with this, but I was willing to play along. "I would say so, yes."

"Model type? Or girl next door?"

"Half and half. Skinny. Blonde. Pretty. Looks quite good in a skirt. Even by L.A. standards."

"Hmmm. Well, no restraining order was ever filed against a Michael Sullivan by Kerrie Edwards in L.A. county."

"What?" I couldn't believe it. Normally I was pretty good at spotting liars and crazy people. And I'd convinced myself that it had been Sullivan in that Mustang. "Could it have been in an adjacent county?"

He wasn't done. "I did, however, find a restraining order against a certain Michael Sullivan, with the correct date of birth, by one Edward Kerry. Same date of birth as your client."

I sat in my chair blinking for what I'm sure was quite some time. "What?" I said again.

I could hear him grinning. "So I dug a little deeper, and found he had his name legally changed about two months later. Roughly eight months ago."

I leaned back in my chair. "Wow. Just...wow."

"Other than the restraining order, that's it. No further criminal or civil legal actions involving either one of them."

"Um. I.... Uhhh...."

"Could've fooled you, huh?" He chuckled. "I'll fax you a copy of everything I found. Listen, I'm not sure just how up-to-speed you people in the Motor City are on this kind of thing, but transitioning is not something that happens overnight. Whether it's male to female or vice versa—"

"There's a vice versa?"

He laughed at my tone. "Oh yeah. But you don't just flip a switch and *Shazam!*, you're Cher. Even after you've decided to take the plunge, so to speak, there are usually interviews with psychologists, and then even if they never get any kind of surgery there's hormones, all sorts of hormones. For years. Maybe for the rest of their life."

I thought about that. "So you're saying this was all going on when the restraining order was signed?"

"Yep. Seems reasonable to think there might be a lot of intense emotions flying about between two people who were close when something like this was going on. That's a big change. Big big change. Especially if they were intimate."

"This is not how I expected this phone call to go," I told him.

"Life's like that. I'll send you a bill."

One great thing about going through a divorce, it really opens up your evenings.

I was hitting the gym about five times a week, usually after leaving the office. After doing my standard hour-long chest and shoulder workout using a few machines but mostly free weights, I got on a treadmill and jogged a slow four miles, then ran half a mile as fast as I could. The half mile kicked my ass more than the four before it had.

Afterward I headed home without showering. There were two reasons for that: 1. after a number of issues in the Army I won't let my bare feet touch a communal shower, bathroom, or locker room floor, and 2. the workout bag I kept with me as I moved from machine to bench to machine contained a pistol, something I didn't like to store even in a padlocked locker. I could defeat a padlock in five seconds.

Home, currently, was an apartment with a kitchen less than two miles from my office. I was going month-to-month on it. A lot of my stuff was still at the house, and I'd only taken a few necessities with me to the apartment. I hadn't really been thrown out of the house, I'd left on my own.

Too many bad memories. Too many dead bodies. Kelly had moved out not long after me—apparently she couldn't take the ghosts either.

Cooking isn't a hard skill to learn, but you have to be interested in the result to do it well. I didn't care to cook for myself, so on the way home I stopped and grabbed a pizza. That was enough of an insult to my body after my workout that I kept away from the bottles of beer I had in the refrigerator and instead just filled a big plastic cup with water from the tap. For all the problems Detroit and its environs have, we've got some of if not the best tap water in the country. Better than some bottled water. I have no idea why.

After eating I hit the shower, then sat back down with Hemingway. Hemingway deliberately wrote with a curt, brusque style, and I'd loved *For Whom the Bell Tolls* and *Green Hills of Africa*, but I really wasn't enjoying *Islands in the Stream*. I ground away at it anyway, doing my best to keep myself a well-rounded individual. I reached the end of the first book in the novel, 'Bimini', where the main character, Thomas Hudson, gets a telegram, without warning, informing him two of his children were killed in a car accident. I stared at the book in my hand for a good thirty seconds, then threw it across the room.

At eleven I flipped on the local news, checking to see if anything important had happened before heading to bed. Channel 7, the local ABC affiliate, did another story on the Mitton case. There didn't seem to be anything new on the story, but they were loving the fact that one of Detroit's upstanding rich white guys had a secret mistress. They showed a photo of her, as well as file footage of Mitton and his wife at a black-tie charity event several years earlier.

I sat up and cocked my head like a dog listening to a distant whistle as the TV anchor moved on to another story.

I'd never seen video of her before meeting Mrs. Mitton, just photos, and hadn't seen her since the visit to my office over six months earlier. She'd had her arm hooked through her husband's as they walked across a marble-floored rotunda somewhere downtown. There was something about that brief video clip that bothered me…. Whatever it was, I couldn't put my finger on it. After a few minutes I left it alone and went to bed.

Chapter Seven

"How much of my retainer do you have left?" Kerrie Edwards asked me three days after I'd lost the Mustang. She'd had time to kill after work before heading to class, and we were having coffee at Starbucks. She was wearing a white silk blouse over tight jeans and heels. She looked great. I kept glancing at her, trying not to be obvious, trying to spot something, but there was just nothing there. No sign she'd ever been anything but the pretty young lady sitting before me. My brain was having a hard time processing the situation, because what my brain now knew about her did not correspond to what I was seeing. Which was why it kept inserting the pronouns 'she' and 'her' whenever I looked at her.

"None."

Her face fell. "Oh."

I took a sip of coffee. "But I'm the idiot that lost him the one time I spotted him, got pulled over by the cops. So I owe you at least a little more time on it."

"I can pay you more. My mom gave me some money.

Another five hundred dollars. She never liked him." She sipped at her coffee and left a faint lipstick mark on the plastic lid.

"Was she in California too?"

"She came and visited, once." She made a face. "That didn't go well."

"Were you transitioning at the time?" I asked. I was genuinely curious. I hadn't meant to ask, but the question just popped out of my mouth.

She blinked at me, frowned, opened and closed her mouth, but didn't say anything. Her face remained blank. I could see the wheels turning.

"I got a copy of the restraining order, hoping there might be something there I could use to find him here." I shrugged. "Relationships are tough at the best of times. I don't really know anything about…it, but I imagine if you add that into the mix even a stable relationship could get a bit rocky."

She didn't know what to say, and sipped at her coffee to buy time. She finally said, "He…he didn't want me to. Thought it was a mistake. We were happy, why ruin a good thing? But he was the happy one, I was always…." She sighed. "Are you gay?" she asked me. I shook my head.

"Gay couples in L.A are everywhere. Not nearly as much as San Francisco, but they're accepted. Have a big public presence. Community. Much more than here. But people like me…once you commit, and start to transition, all of a sudden a lot of those people who were on your team suddenly won't answer the phone. Our suicide rate is through the roof because of that, among other reasons, but nobody wants to talk about that. If you look like a girl, gay guys generally have zero romantic interest. You'll get some one-night stands, because you're a curiosity, a freak, like fucking a midget—"

Her voice had been rising as she got angry, and she visibly calmed herself. She looked around to see if anyone was paying attention, then went on. "Straight guys won't have anything to do with you if they know, they're afraid the gay will rub off on them or something. If you're trying to date and you keep it a secret, and the guy finds out because you're pre-op or whatever, you're likely to get punched in the face, if not worse. So, you're marooned, and sometimes it seems like the only people who care about you, who have an idea what you're going through, are the ones just like you." She gave a bitter sigh. "And we're a small, strange little club, let me tell you. Shit, I thought Mikey loved me. Loved me for who I was. On the inside, not my body. And on the inside, I feel like a girl. Pretty much always have. Did the whole time we were together. I thought he knew that. But he wanted to have a boyfriend. Because, you know, he was in love with a man. He was gay, he didn't want to walk around and be seen with a…with a girl." She shook her head. "We argued and fought so much. He was against it. Said it was wrong for me. Turns out it was more about what he wanted, him wanting to control me than anything else. But once he drove me away he lost control, and that drove him a little crazy, I guess." She looked at me and gave a little laugh. "I've had bad breakups before, but nothing like this. You?"

I took a slow sip of coffee and shrugged. "I'm in the middle of a divorce. We can't talk for two minutes without us screaming at each other." Further details were none of her business, and to be honest many of them were covered by the non-disclosure agreement I'd signed. We both sat quiet for a time. "Love sucks," I said finally. "Because then you care that they hate you."

"What are you doing?" Jerry sounded cheerful. It made me want to punch him through the phone.

"Regretting a lot of the choices I've made in my life."

"You feeling suicidal? Do I need to drive over there and jump in front of your gun?" He was joking, but I could hear the concern in his voice. I sighed.

"I can think of at least fifty people I'd kill before I'd kill myself," I told him. "I've got a list, just in case I get inoperable cancer or something."

"Am I on the list?"

"Yeah, but you're way down there, I don't think you even made the top twenty." I blew air out and sat up. "Just sitting here staring at Kerrie Edwards' car, waiting for her to get out of class." The sun had dipped behind a low bank of clouds on the horizon, but the sky was still bright. Pure, deep ocean blue. Both the temperature and humidity had dropped, and it was a beautiful summer evening. Which I was spending sitting in my car in a parking lot.

"I can't believe you blew through a red light right in front of a cop. That's a rookie move." I'd told him about spotting the Mustang, or at least a Mustang, then had to explain how my pursuit had been aborted before I was able to make a positive ID.

"Don't make me regret telling you." My eyes dropped down to the passenger seat. The now three-day-old Detroit News was still there, folded to show the photo of Mitton's mistress and her lawyer. Everyone seemed to be unlucky in love these days. At least she was getting a chunk of cash for her troubles. A big chunk. "Why are you calling?"

"Because I'm not independently wealthy."

"You have more cash than most people your age. You have more cash than most people, period." Jerry's parents had hired me two years earlier to find him when he'd gone missing. He hadn't been kidnapped, he was in hiding because he'd witnessed a murder. His friends had bullied their way into my investigation—luckily, otherwise I probably would have ended up dead—and in the process recovered a big chunk of cash whose owners were no longer among the living. Split four ways it was still six figures for each of them. And none of them had done anything stupid with it to draw the attention of the IRS, which I counted as some kind of minor miracle. Then again, none of them was anywhere close to dumb.

"I have no idea what you're talking about," he said, and I could hear the smile. "But I would still like to work tomorrow."

He was hinting at something, but—"Shit, I was supposed to email you that case."

"Bingo."

I glanced into the backseat. I had my laptop with me. "Let me see if I can jump onto somebody's Wi-Fi here. Maybe the school's got an unsecured connection. If not, I'll send it when I get home." I grabbed the laptop, flipped it open, and turned it on. It always took forever to boot up.

"If you don't, I'm calling you when I get up at oh-dark-thirty tomorrow. Assuming it's got a six a.m. start?"

"I...don't remember."

"What the hell were you doing today that's got you so distracted?"

"Not shooting people who annoyed me." I shifted in my seat as my SIG was digging into my hipbone. "I'm hanging up now."

The college did have a Wi-Fi signal, and it seemed to be unsecured, which I was both glad and disgusted to see. "Unsecured Wi-Fi is a security risk" didn't have the same ring as "loose lips sink ships", but come on, we were at war with a sizable chunk of the world, and a public community college didn't even have a password set up to secure internet access to their network?

"Morons," I swore, and looked up from my computer to see the back end of a car sliding out the far end of the lot. A square back end. That looked a lot like an older Mustang. It was too dark to be sure of the color, but...

"Shit," I swore, and tossed the laptop onto the seat beside me.

I caught up to the vehicle as it was waiting to turn left onto Farmington Road. It was a late eighties Mustang, and its arresting blue color was still obvious even as the sun sank behind the horizon. Through the tint I could barely make out the silhouette of whoever was behind the wheel—it was a guy, but that was all I was sure of. But I got the license plate.

Farmington Road wasn't too busy at that hour, but there was only one lane in each direction. He turned, heading south, and I had to wait for two more cars to pass by before I could pull out. I didn't mind; the cars gave me cover.

Most everyone had their headlights on, but it wasn't truly dark yet, dusk was still creeping in. While the road was lined with trees it was an illusion; the area was thick with upper-middle-class suburbs hidden just out of sight.

Two miles down Farmington dead-ended at Shiawassee. If he wanted to stay headed south on Farmington he'd have to turn right and pick it up a thousand feet down. Instead, he turned left, and followed Shiawassee through neighborhoods and the occasional

Splits and Transitions

business until it hit Orchard Lake Road. I assumed he would turn right, as turning left would send him north, heading back the way we'd come. So I was surprised when he got into the left turn lane. I was already drifting over to the right lane.

"Shit." It was a common refrain when I was following people, even when things were going well.

I turned right just a few seconds after he turned left. I immediately pulled into the parking lot of an office building, threw a U-turn, and nosed out onto Orchard Lake. The Mustang was a few hundred yards up in the left lane. I pulled out, paused just a second for the northbound light to change, then roared after the vehicle, staying in the right lane.

Following people for dummies:

1. Never be directly behind someone you're following if you can help it. Be in a different lane and if you can't do that, use distance or other cars to separate yourself.

2. Try to never make two turns in a row while directly behind the subject.

3. Shut off your damn daytime running lights if you're stuck with a car that has them.

After two miles the Mustang was nearing the east exit of the college campus. There was absolutely no reason for him to have driven in the big circle I'd followed him through, but I'd long ago stopped trying to guess why the people I was following were doing what they were doing. There could have been any number of reasons. I hadn't done anything to draw attention to my vehicle, and I'd only been directly behind him for one turn, so I doubted that he'd even noticed my Tahoe.

Have I mentioned how I haven't been having a great deal of luck following people lately?

Past Ten Mile Road he was in the left lane. Half a mile ahead the road went over I-696. The eastbound on-ramp was on the right, and to access the westbound ramp he'd have to cross over the freeway and turn left. I slowed down and was almost a quarter mile back, and in the right lane, when he hammered it.

I saw the back end of the Mustang dip half a second before I heard the roar of the exhaust. He swerved around a slow-moving Camry then sharply veered right, taking the eastbound on-ramp at double the posted limit.

My Tahoe had a big engine, but it was also a big, heavy SUV and cornered like a drunken toaster. By the time I pushed it hard through the curve of the ramp the Mustang was just a dim spot half a mile up on the freeway. He'd extinguished his headlights, making him much harder to spot, and was slaloming through the slower cars. I floored it, but he was out of sight within fifteen seconds. He had to be doing well over triple digits. I kept at it for a couple miles, pushing my Chevy to the ragged edge, hoping to spot him at the top of a ramp exiting the freeway, but no such luck.

I slowed to ten over the speed limit (which is slow for 696) and called my client. "Are you still in class?"

"No, I'm driving, I just got done. I'm heading home. Why?"

"Meet me at that McDonald's by your house, on Big Beaver, before you go home," I told her.

A quick pass through her neighborhood showed me the usual—no sign of the Mustang. I parked in the strip mall lot, found some unsecured Wi-Fi, and accessed the

Michigan Secretary of State database. The SOS was Michigan's DMV, and I ran the plate on the Mustang. It came back to a 1996 Chevy station wagon (SOS-speak for an SUV) registered to Marion Winchester of Harrison Township, which was northeast of Detroit along Lake St. Clair. Frowning and thinking in equal measure I drove over to the McDonald's parking lot and waited.

Kerrie Edwards pulled up next to my vehicle and rolled down her window. "What's going on?"

"He was at the school tonight."

She blinked. "He was?"

"Had to be. Late eighties Mustang. One guy inside. Drove through your lot, and even though I never did anything to spook him he took off like a bat out of hell." That's what had convinced me it was Sullivan in the Mustang. Unless he'd been looking for surveillance he never would have spotted me, and only people up to no good are watching for a tail. "I just couldn't keep up, that thing's not just a fancy paint job, he's got a monster under the hood. Plate comes back to an SUV, maybe stolen. You ever hear the name Marion Winchester?"

She shook her head. "No. Who's that?"

"That's who the plate belongs to. Harrison Township, although the plate could have been stolen anywhere." I made a face. "This technically doesn't change anything, but…he's skittish, real skittish, to have keyed on me. And so now we add that to the mix. You pay attention. Look around the house and up and down the street whenever you're leaving or getting home, or work, or school. And if you see anything hinky, you call me if I'm there, but otherwise the police, you don't chance it."

She'd gone pale. "Okay."

Chapter Eight

I followed Kerrie from home to work in the morning, but there was no sign of Sullivan. I'd been at my office for an hour when my phone rang.

"Mr. Phault?"

"That'd be me."

"'Phault Investigations and Security'. You're a private investigator?"

His tone made me cock my head and sit up. "Yes sir. How can I help you?"

"This is Sergeant Randolph Parker with the Michigan State Police. Did you run a license plate last night using your business account with the Secretary of State?" He read me the plate off Sullivan's Mustang.

"Yeah. Let me guess, it was stolen."

"Why do you say that?"

Cops, always interrogating everyone. Always assuming everyone is lying to them. Unfortunately, that's because they usually are.

Splits and Transitions

"Because it came back to a '96 SUV and was on a late eighties Mustang."

"Why were you running the plate, sir?"

"I've got a case. A stalker. The victim is my client. That plate was on the Mustang belonging to the ex, who has been following her. Followed her all the way from LA. He never registered the vehicle here, so it makes sense he slapped a stolen tag on it. Took off when he suspected someone was behind him."

"Who's your client?"

I smiled. "I can't tell you that, but I can tell you all the juicy details of the guy following her. And give you a good description of the vehicle, not that that will help you much. I don't know where he's staying, he's got no local ties. Up 'til last night he's been a ghost. How long ago was the plate stolen?"

He grunted. "No way to know. The complainant noticed it three days ago. Does your client live in Harrison Township?"

"Troy. Any other license plates stolen in the area?"

"Not that anyone's noticed. Yet."

I shrugged. "Sorry I couldn't be more help."

He sighed. "Just dotting the i's. Mostly it's kids who steal these, but when you ran it it popped up in the system. So… this guy pursued her from California, and is now stealing plates to stick on his vehicle so he can follow her?"

"Looks like."

"Oh boy. That's not nothing. She own a gun?" He knew anyone crazy enough to do everything Sullivan had done wouldn't be deterred by a piece of paper. Exactly what I'd told Kerrie Edwards.

"Already had that discussion with her. She can't bear the thought of shooting someone."

"Well then, hopefully she's got nine-one-one on speed dial. Give me what info you have on him, and his car. Maybe somebody will get lucky."

It was getting late enough in the morning that I was starting to think about what I wanted for lunch when I heard the office door open.

"Hello?"

I got no response, just the sound of steps. Then Scott Copley appeared, and sat in the client's chair across the desk from me. We stared at each other for a while. He looked the way I felt.

"I don't want to talk about it," I said finally. I've known Scott since junior high school. He was Best Man at my wedding. I'd only spoken to him—very briefly—two or maybe three times in the past six months. None of those conversations had ended well. He was currently a Lieutenant with the Oakland Country Sheriff's Department, and knew a lot of my secrets. But not all of them.

His face got red and he visibly fought down some anger. "That's obvious, but you need to," he told me. "That's pretty fucking obvious too. And I'm not going to take no for a fucking answer. Not any more. You show up at midnight with your pregnant wife covered in blood, tell me to send her out of town, and then both of you disappear for a month. Christmas, New Year's, nothing. Suddenly you're back. She's not pregnant, and you're living in a hotel. And not just living in a hotel, not in fucking jail. After stacking a bunch of bodies. All of you. Grinnand beheaded a guy on camera, for God's sake. I assume he's in jail, and I'm glad you're not, but seriously, what the fuck? I covered for you. Talk to me. What happened with you and Kelly? She won't return my calls either." He stared at me, now more sad than angry.

"Scott, I—"

"Don't tell me you don't want to talk about it," he spat.

"I can't talk about it!" I nearly screamed at him. "Don't you get it? I can't! I signed an NDA."

He blinked and sat back. He opened and closed his mouth a few times. "An...an NDA? With who?" I could see his mind racing.

"I can't tell you that either." He probably wouldn't have believed me if I had. "I'm violating the NDA just by telling you it exists."

We sat and stared at each other for a long time. He knew about some of the bodies I'd dropped. Knew the very fact some sort of non-disclosure agreement existed meant there was a lot going on that he didn't know about. "Are you wanted by anyone?"

"Didn't you run me?" I smiled thinly.

He nodded. "Yeah."

I spread my arms. "Free and clear."

He blinked twice. "All of you?" I nodded. "Grinnand?" he asked dubiously, expecting me to say no.

"All of us," I told him.

"He cut a guy's head off!"

"Someone pretending to be an FBI agent," I said slowly, doing my best not to tell him anything that wasn't already known to local law enforcement. "Five someones, actually, if you remember. Armed. Trying to abduct him. All of them with perfect fake creds. And they'd just killed his fiancée."

We sat there for a while, me waiting while he thought. Probably working through various scenarios in his head. He wasn't dumb, and would know that between the dead fake FBI agents, the NDA, and the lack of criminal charges, this had to reach way up the federal food chain. And he'd be right, but as to how high it reached in government his imagination was probably lacking. "Did Kelly lose the baby?" he finally asked me, voice quiet.

I just nodded. I didn't trust myself to speak. He could see how my face went flat at the question.

"She blame you?"

I just stared at him. Finally, he sighed. "Christ, no wonder you're so fucked up. And the dog too, I almost forgot about that. She loved that dog like it was a person. You guys trying to work it out?"

"She's filed for divorce. Nothing I do or say has been able to change her mind." I choked back something trying to spill out of my mouth, and instead said, "She won't talk to me anymore. Everything has to go through our lawyers."

"You still in a hotel? She still at the house?"

I shook my head. "Too many bad memories for both of us there. I'm in an apartment nearby. She got one in downtown Rochester. Probably sell the house once the divorce goes through, split the money." I made a face.

"Jesus, John." He stared out my window for a while. "You want to go to lunch, somewhere that serves alcohol, and get really drunk?"

"It wouldn't be the worst decision I've made this week."

Chapter Nine

Nursing a not-inconsiderable hangover the next morning, I cruised up and down the streets of Harrison Township, looking for Sullivan's Mustang.

Harrison Township was shaped like a fat wedge of pie, with the point heading out into Lake St. Clair. It was split in two by the Clinton River, and most of the north half of the city was taken up by Selfridge Air National Guard Base. The Lake St. Clair Metropark, known to all the locals as Metro Beach, took up most of the tip, so in fact there weren't many streets in the city—after subtracting the military base and the park, maybe four or five square miles of actual residential land.

All I'd accomplished the day before was repairing my friendship with Scott, although that was no little thing. However, as punishment for getting drunk and wasting most of the previous day I vowed to drive up and down every street in the city, looking for the Mustang. In all honesty it didn't take me very long.

Most of the houses had garages, and most of those were

closed. A number of the houses on the east side of the city were situated on canals, and a bit pricey because of that—I didn't see Sullivan shacking up in one of them, but I drove up and down those streets too.

Of course I never spotted his car, but I had to try.

I parked my Tahoe in front of a long low ranch with an attached two car garage on Villa Mar Street. The house had an off-white brick and flagstone exterior, with white trim. There was a twenty-foot motorboat on a trailer in the circular driveway in front of the house, and the garage door was up. There was a canal directly behind the house, and each house seemed to have its own boat slip.

"Can I help you?"

I pulled down my sunglasses and saw a thick sixty-something man in the garage, wiping his hands on a rag.

"Mr. Winchester?"

"That'd be me." He moved to the edge of the garage, staying in the shade. His glasses reflected the bright sunlight. It made my throbbing brain ache.

"I'm a private investigator. I'm actually here about the license plate you had stolen."

He looked surprised. "Private investigator? Don't know that I've ever actually met one before in real life. Are you working the case? I thought it was a police thing."

"It is. State Police are working it. But I was following the person who probably stole your wife's plate and stuck it on his car, and I had a couple of questions."

"It was my plate." He stuck a thumb at himself. "Marion Winchester. Lot of people make that mistake. O-N is a man's name, A-N is usually a woman."

I nodded. "Marion Morrison. I should have known better, sorry."

His face brightened at the mention of someone who got

quite famous using the name John Wayne. "That's right. Not many people remember that, these days. So how can I help you?"

"Just trying to track down the guy who stole your plate. For another case I'm working." I waved a hand around the neighborhood. Villa Mar was a short, dead-end street in the middle of a neighborhood that wasn't on the way to anywhere. "Not exactly a high traffic area. Not where I would go if I was going to steal a plate. The trooper said you didn't know when it had been stolen, but was it likely to have been stolen here? Was the car parked in the garage, or in the driveway or street? Do you drive it to work?" I looked around. "I don't see it."

"It's my son's car. Ninety-six Blazer. Parks it in the driveway. He goes to U of M, but he's been home for the summer for a month or so. He's working right now."

"Where does he work?"

"The Kroger at Thirteen and Gratiot. He's a cashier." He shrugged. "I don't know, but if I had to guess the plate was probably stolen there. He works nights, two or three times a week."

"You ever seen a late-eighties electric blue Mustang around here?"

He shook his head. "Can't say I have. But almost nobody drives down this street who doesn't live here. It's quiet. That's why we like it."

The Kroger was not quite four miles away, at the southwest corner of a very busy intersection, less than half a mile from an on-ramp to I-94. It was the anchor store in a short strip mall with a DSW, a Hobby Lobby, and a Best Buy. There were two restaurants between the retail stores and Gratiot, adding to the traffic. I found what was probably the Winchester's Blazer parked in the lot—there was a temporary paper plate taped to the rear window—and did a perfunctory pass through the lot. If I was looking for a busy lot where I could steal a plate without being noticed and quickly jump onto the freeway to put distance between myself and the scene of the crime, I doubt I could have picked a better spot.

Still, it wasn't a random spot. Sullivan didn't drive across half the state to steal a plate off a car in that lot, he was familiar with the area. Which meant he was living, or maybe working, nearby. But half a million people lived in the south end of Macomb county. Driving around and trying to spot him would be like trying to find a needle in a haystack.

I'd been expecting the phone to ring for a long time before it actually did. I muted my TV before I answered. I checked my watch. Just before eleven p.m.

"You know," Jerry said into my ear without preamble, "I lost my virginity when I was sixteen. In college I was in a threesome."

"Ummm…" I said, frowning, but he kept going

"I've been kidnapped, I helped torture a man, I've been in gun fights, *plural*, I've even met the President. Not that I can tell anyone, or that they'd believe me if I did. I considered myself worldly. But, apparently, I'm still naïve."

"Is this going somewhere? What happened?" Another Friday had rolled around, and I'd had him working the William Kern case with Mike. Jerry's Explorer, with its V-8, was the fastest car any of us had, and after losing Kern once I didn't want it happening again.

"It just never occurred to me that there were gay bars in Detroit," he said.

"Oh God." A lead weight hit my gut. "What happened?"

Jerry sounded cheerful. "He drove like a bat out of hell, again. After grabbing what looked like another bottle of wine out of his trunk. I think he was working up some liquid courage before heading out. And I'm pretty sure it was wine. Because he wasn't just driving fast, he was driving sloppy. First we went to the Gold Coast. Mike told me it was a gay bar. I didn't believe him. He was only inside half an hour. Then we went to Menjo's."

The lead weight in my stomach dragged it lower. "That's probably the most famous gay bar in Detroit," I told him.

"Yeah, and like I said, it never occurred to me that there were *any* gay bars in Detroit. Currently," he told me, "we are at the Male Box. That's M-A-L-E. Two words. On Seven Mile. It's wet jockeys night here."

I frowned and cocked my head. "You mean like jockey shorts? Underpants?"

"It's the gay guy equivalent of a wet t-shirt contest, apparently," he told me. "Who knew? Not me. He's been inside about forty-five minutes."

"Did you go inside?"

"No," he said quickly. "Mike and I are still out in the parking lot. He's been talking to the security guard who keeps an eye on the cars and the lot. If you want me to go inside, as young and handsome as I am…I'm going to need combat pay."

"You think you're going to get hit on? You should be so lucky." Then I shut my mouth and engaged my brain. "Wow," I said. "Just…wow." And paused for a long time, thinking. "Christ," I finally said. "I've got to call the client."

"Better you than me. What do you want us to do?"

If William Kern stopped at just one such establishment, it wouldn't be hard to argue or imagine that he hadn't known it catered to a certain clientele. But three? "Just stay there. I assume you're done, but I'll get back to you." I got serious. "And if I need you to go in to get eyeballs on him, you're going in."

"Yeah, I know. Whatever you need."

I called Jerry back ten minutes later. "Okay, you're done. Tell Mike."

"How did she take it?" he asked.

"She was devastated." As I knew she'd be as soon as I'd heard Kern was hitting gay bars. I felt nearly as bad as she did. "She'd thought she'd internalized the idea that he was cheating on her. Which is one whole kind of betrayal. But the fact that he's hiding much more than that was honestly more than she was ready to handle. Now she's thinking back, wondering just how much of their relationship, their marriage, was a lie."

"Do they have kids? I'm just wondering if he's always been gay, or bi, or whatever, and just hid it from her, or this is something that happened later..."

"I think she's asking herself those same questions. I don't know. I don't think they have kids."

He didn't speak for a while, then he finally said, "Well, I don't know if that's better or worse."

Chapter Ten

Melinda Rogers lived on the west side of Detroit, maybe a mile in a straight line from downtown. Her house was the fifth from the end of the block, a cube-ish two-story with a raised, covered porch that had probably been built in in the 1940s, when Detroit was the greatest manufacturing center in the history of the world. There was a detached two-car garage behind the house whose door had been closed when I arrived at six a.m. and which had still been closed when I did a drive-by just before nine a.m.

She had only one car registered to her, and reportedly lived alone but for two minor children, so I didn't have to sit close enough to eyeball her specific driveway. Which was lucky, as the block was packed shoulder-to-shoulder with houses similar to hers, and only a couple of them appeared to be vacant. More houses meant more eyes on my vehicle. If they knew one of their neighbors was out on comp, lots of people in the hood, if they spotted a strange blacked-out vehicle on the street, would call the claimant to warn her or him about potential surveillance. I've had it happen more than once.

I parked on the next block south, where there wouldn't be so many eyeballs, and where the claimant wouldn't be able to see my vehicle unless she walked out into her front yard and looked down the street. And if she did that, I was probably already blown. The west side of the street opposite me had almost a full contingent of houses, although a quarter of them appeared empty. The east side of the street was completely devoid of houses, all of them having been torn down by the city at some point in the near or distant past. This early in the summer the grass was only about knee high. South of me the block ended abruptly, the street having to do a sharp right turn before a double set of raised train tracks.

Unfortunately, the spot where I elected to park had no shade whatsoever. I'd shut off my engine and cracked my windows, but the temperature was rising to the point where I'd be forced to turn on my air conditioning. My mood wasn't helped when my phone rang.

"I thought we'd agreed that all communication would go through me, or my office." My divorce lawyer, Reginald J. Beeman—never Reggie, and only R.J. to his friends—sounded very put out.

"Yeah, well, I was just trying to talk to her about—" He cut me off.

"During our last conference call with her and her lawyer it was made very clear to me, to you, to God himself, that she did not want to talk to you directly. About anything." He clucked. "While divorce itself is an extenuating circumstance that the judge should take into account, I do not see it outside the realm of possibility that if you persist in contacting, or trying to contact her, that she goes to the courthouse to secure a personal protection order against you. If that happens, I believe it voids your concealed pistol license. You would be unable to carry a gun. Legally. Which, based on what I've come to know about you, would be very upsetting."

I sighed. Loudly. "Beeman," I began. Again he cut me off.

"I have extended this process as much as I am able," he told me, "and enjoyed billing you for it, but the truth of the matter is that it is over but for the dust settling. We have an appointment in front of the judge in a few weeks. At that time, the judgement of divorce will be signed and it will be over. The only way that won't happen is if your wife changes her mind. And that is the only way. Do you see that happening? Even if you were able to speak to her at length, in person?"

He knew what had happened between the two of us. I opened and closed my mouth a few times. Finally, I said, "No."

"Then we are agreed. Let it happen. Be sad. Be happy. Get drunk. Eat a gallon of ice cream. But don't call her, or you're likely to find yourself on the wrong end of a PPO."

Just after ten a.m. my phone rang again. I was still in a bad mood, but recognized the number. "Mr. Phault? Michelle Cleary, Shelby-Haund."

Michelle, and Shelby-Haund Services Inc., the "Premier Claims Services Provider", sent me a lot of insurance cases. As adjusters went she was better than most and usually great to work with. "Good morning Michelle. What's up?"

"Well, ah, I've been going over your latest surveillance report on Louis Brown with the insured, and, um, they're hoping you can edit it." She sounded uncomfortable.

I blinked and sat up a little. "Edit it how?"

"Do you have a copy of the report with you?"

"I'm sorry, I don't. I'm on a surveillance right now."

"Well, perhaps I could read it to you, to refresh your memory?"

"That'd be fine."

"You were doing surveillance on Tuesday, May thirteenth. At ten-oh-three you wrote, quote, "A blue Pontiac Grand Prix, license plate X1F 55E parked on the street in front of the claimant's house. The driver and sole occupant was a middle-aged male of apparent Mediterranean descent. He walked up to the claimant's door and knocked. The claimant answered and the male went inside. Video was obtained."

I remembered. It was about the only thing that had happened in two days of surveillance on Mr. Brown, who was reportedly suffering from a bad knee. "Right. Is there a problem?"

"Well, um, they are not comfortable with your description."

I frowned. "My description? Of the car or the visitor?"

"The visitor."

My frown got deeper. "Perhaps I'm running a little slow today. Do they not like the middle-aged part, or the Mediterranean part?"

She blew out a breath. "The Mediterranean part. They're wondering if you can change that."

"I was actually pretty happy with that description," I told her. "You've seen the video. The guy could be Italian. He could be Greek. Maybe Spanish. Caucasian features, but a little too tan, and his hair was blacker than black. Probably not north African, or the Balkan states, but you never know. 'Apparent Mediterranean descent' was the best generic description I could come up with that was accurate."

"Yes, well, this client has become very particular about the wording in their surveillance reports. In all their paperwork, actually. I wanted to talk to you about Donte Ferguson as well. You did a one-day surveillance on him last week."

"Donte. I remember it well. I remember him well. You and I already had a discussion about how doing surveillance on that guy is just asinine and a total waste of money. I don't know what the client is thinking. He lost a finger. A thumb, in fact. Amputated at work in a bad accident, in front of ten witnesses. Non-recoverable. If the insured thinks he's faking, just send him to an IME and have the doctor count his fingers. Any number higher than nine is fraud. Doing surveillance on him seems more like harassment than anything else. The dude is just trying to get his real estate license now, and you don't need two thumbs to show houses. But anyway, what's the issue with the report?"

"Ummm, when you first saw him, and he walked to the corner store. You described him as a black male. The client has asked that we use the term African-American. They've asked that we make those changes to the surveillance reports going forward."

I got my temper under control before I spoke, but just barely.

"Whoa whoa whoa," I said, "time out. First off, I know you know this, but I'm going to repeat it anyway. If you're editing my reports before you give them to the client, be aware that if I'm ever called to testify on one of these cases, I'm going to use *my* copy of the report, and if the defense ever learns you've edited one of those reports, that their copy differs from the original in any way, they're going to eat your lunch. And the magistrate will hand them a napkin."

Her voice was bitter. "I'm aware of that. And I've said as much to my supervisors. They seem more worried about losing a big client."

"Second, I understand the lure of politically correct terms. Everybody wants to get along, be one big happy. And I will happily use politically correct terms in my reports, provided they are technically accurate politically correct terms. Unfortunately, most politically correct terms are not factually correct. I write my reports assuming that, at some point, I will have to testify in court as to their contents and my actions on the day in question. So I do my damndest to keep out opinions and feelings and guesses, and only describe in those reports what I observed, to the best of my ability. If I, in fact, described Mr. Ferguson as an African-American, I would be making an assumption about his heritage. And in this case I'd be wrong. The client should know that."

I shook my head and stared out the windshield, not seeing anything. "Check out that recorded statement he gave last year, it's in the file. Ferguson is Dominican. He came over when he was three with his parents. Neither of whom are African. Ferguson mentioned somewhere in the reports you gave me his ancestors originally came from Cuba. So his family's Caribbean, through and through. If I start making assumptions of ancestry in my reports, one day I'm going to be totally wrong, and on that day I am going to be eaten alive on the stand. 'Black' is a physical descriptor and covers Dominican, Haitian, African, American, some Brazilians, maybe a few Egyptians, everyone with dark skin."

I smiled thinly. "Anyway, I understand people want to

play nice and be socially responsible and warm and fuzzy, but you're not the one who has to testify, in court, under oath, to what you wrote in these reports. I do." I took a deep breath, trying to calm myself. Keep my voice low and even. "If I find out that you're altering my reports before submitting them to the insured so that they don't contain any words they don't like, I can no longer work for your company, as we will have lost trust. You can trust that I will accurately describe what I see. Or don't see. If that means you can no longer use me or my firm, so be it." I found I was sweating, my face hot.

"I understand. I will bring this up to Larry." She sighed. "Again. You're not telling me anything I haven't already told him. Several times. I'll let you know."

"Thanks. Sorry for yelling." I was still mad, but it wasn't her fault. No need to take it out on her.

"No, I get it. And this isn't the only issue we're dealing with. Some of the doctors doing our IMEs are getting pressure from the carriers to not describe patients as 'obese'. Because it's hurtful or something like that. Even when they're clearly big fat pigs, with BMIs of forty or fifty, and, technically, medically, obese is anything over thirty percent body fat." Michelle was a not-unattractive long-distance runner who had no patience for fat people who refused to acknowledge that obesity was self-inflicted.

I caught movement in my rearview mirror and saw a car had pulled around the corner a hundred yards behind me and was heading my way. It wasn't moving fast and began slowing down further.

"Yeah. Again, sorry. Good luck with that," I said distractedly.

The car—it looked like a black Monte Carlo—rolled to a stop about seventy-five feet behind me, halfway down the block, a few feet from the curb. Both the driver and passenger doors opened. The driver was a young black guy and he walked around to the passenger side. I only caught a glimpse of the passenger as he exited the car and seemed to crouch down. The other man joined him, and then suddenly a loud crack rang out. I jumped in my seat as the driver jogged back around the car and jumped behind the wheel. I recognized the sound for what it was—a gunshot, probably a small caliber handgun. Had they just taken a shot at me?

The engine of the Monte roared and the wheels chirped as the driver did a U-turn and took off the way he'd come. I started the Tahoe and took off after them, bouncing over the far curb as my turning radius sucked. I was in third gear, engine straining, when I passed the spot where they'd been briefly parked. I was taking the curve at the end of the block when my brain finished processing what I had seen. The Monte Carlo was half a block ahead of me, slowing for a stop sign, no longer in a hurry.

Seeing red, I roared up on their left side and cut them off in the middle of the intersection and jumped out, gun up. "Let me see your hands! Let me see your hands!" I screamed at them. They stared at me with scared faces. Scared, young, stupid faces. That didn't recognize me.

"Where's the gun?" I shouted, sticking my SIG in the driver's face.

"It's in the glove box, man!" They were shaking.

"What the fuck were you thinking?"

"We was just putting a dog down man, that's all, we weren't bangin'," the passenger said, keeping his hands up. His eyes were wide. They assumed I was a cop.

"That puppy's back there flopping in the gutter!" I screamed, pointing my pistol back the direction we'd come, then back in the driver's face. It couldn't have been more than a few months old and was still fuzzy, where it hadn't been covered in fresh blood. I found myself fighting back tears. "You," I hit him in the chest with the SIG's muzzle with every word, "didn't…put…down…shit. Goddammit!" I straightened up and spun around. I saw a few people on nearby porches, looking our way. At least one of them was on a phone. "FUCK!"

"I might have overreacted," I said quietly to the Sergeant, leaning against his cruiser, my arms crossed. "But I thought they took a shot at me."

I'd been handcuffed, at first, by the first responding officers. Then the Sergeant had rolled up, and after hearing my story, and talking to the two idiots in the Monte Carlo, had uncuffed me. The two of them were still cuffed, in the back seat of the other squad car. We both stared at them. I took a deep breath and let it out.

"You scared the ever-lovin' shit out of them, that's the truth," Sergeant Cooper said. He gave me a direct look. "Good." He cleared his throat. "Discharge of a firearm inside the city limits." He ticked the charges off on his hand as he went. "Weapons charge for the gun in the car. A little Raven .25, no wonder it didn't do the job. Open intoxicants too, they both had beers. Animal cruelty. That's what I can think of off the top of my head. I'm actually shocked we didn't find any weed in that Monte, these two."

"They're just a couple of morons," I said, nearly as disgusted with myself as I was them. And I'd nearly shot them both in a rage.

"Detectives are too busy to come down on something

like this, but they're going to need a statement. Expect a call."

"Yeah. What's the news on the dog?" It had looked like a husky/shepherd mix. Fluffy. Cute, except for all the blood and aimlessly flopping limbs. I clenched my fists and tried to calm down.

He shrugged. "It was still alive when the Humane Society picked it up. But it was shot in the head."

"Shit."

"Yeah. But you never know. Give them a call tomorrow."

Chapter Eleven

"You okay?" Jerry Phillips asked me. "You seem wired."

"Just need to blow off some steam. It's been a bad week. Bad couple of weeks." I paused. "Bad year."

He traded a look with Ron Kelly. We were in the barn at Ron's house, looking out the back. The double door was wide enough for two horses. Most of the ground floor of the barn was taken up by stables, but now that Ron's mother had sold off her horses they were quiet and empty, smelling vaguely of hay, horse, and horseshit.

"I set up an El Prez," Jerry told me. "We can start off just practicing basic stuff, then get fancy if you want."

I stepped out the back door into the sunlight. There were three target stands with carboard silhouettes stapled to them. The targets were a yard apart. Jerry had marked a spot on the grass ten yards from the targets.

The "El Presidente" was perhaps the oldest practical shooting drill meant to test—and judge—your defensive shooting ability with a handgun. Start ten yards from three targets, facing away from them with your hands above your shoulders in what was called "surrender" position. At the start signal, turn, draw your pistol, fire two shots at each target, do a reload, and fire another two shots at each target. The drill was simple, but required a little bit of body movement, a draw, a reload, and firing multiple rounds at multiple targets, pretty much everything you'd want to know how to do if you owned, much less carried, a gun for self-defense. And the drill was timed as well, to add a bit more pressure.

Behind the targets George Kelly had thrown up a six-foot berm with a front-end loader so long ago it was completely covered with grass. Beyond it was property freshly cleared of trees, soon to become a golf course. There was an identical berm to our left, and a hundred feet past it was a line of new and nearly identical houses. Only their roofs were visible.

I went back into the barn and emptied the pistol magazines I had of the premium hollowpoints I carried, and filled them with much less expensive practice ammunition. "That's what you're carrying now?" Ron asked, looking at the SIG P226 on my hip. It was in a Kramer Vertical Scabbard, which was actually made out of horsehide. Horsehide looked like leather, but seemed as hard and durable as plastic.

"Yeah. I loved that 1911 I had last year, but it only holds eight rounds, and I ran dry at the hotel even with two spares." That had been just one of the many gunfights I'd been in on our quest to rescue Ron's father. At the start it had been four on one, until I got a little backup, but I still ran out of ammo. To say I never wanted that to happen again was an understatement.

"SIG holds fifteen. With two reloads," I gestured at the two spare magazines on my left hip, "that give me forty-six rounds." Even if I'd wanted to carry that custom 1911, which had been a birthday gift from the guys, the government had seized it after our adventure had come to an end. And promptly destroyed it, if I had to guess, along with a lot of other evidence.

"Yeah, forty-six rounds of nine millimeter," Jerry said derisively. He was a big bullet fan. .45s.

"Speer Gold Dot has a pretty good street record. 124-grain +Ps," I told him.

"I'm just giving you shit," he said, smiling. "You ready to go?"

"Sure." I put in earplugs, then donned shooting glasses. Normally I carry my gun concealed, but for my first run at least I took off the stiff cotton work shirt I had covering it. I loaded the SIG, hit the decocker, and stuck it back in the holster, which Jerry had recommended.

I turned my back to the targets, raised my hands, and nodded at Jerry. He raised an electronic timer that heard and recorded the shots down to one-hundredth of a second. He gave me formal range commands. "Shooter ready? Stand by." He hit the button on the timer and it gave a loud beep. I turned, drew, fired two aimed shots at the center of each of the three targets, reloaded with a spare mag from my belt without any fumbling, and fired two more shots at each of the targets.

"Eight point two two seconds," Jerry said. He peered at the targets. "All A-zone hits. Not bad. You can shoot that thing, but that new hammer spring helps, huh?" He turned to Ron. "The factory hammer spring on that SIG is strong enough to send a man into orbit. I put a reduced power one in there, it took two pounds off the double action trigger pull and a pound off the single, while still being just as reliable."

Jerry turned to me. "You have enough ammo on you to do it again? Let's try something. You need to work on your splits and transitions."

"My what?" He was an avid competition shooter and often used terms that left me in the dark.

"Your splits are the times between shots on the same target. Your transitions are the times between shots as you transition between different targets." He pointed downrange. "When you shot, you went bang-bang, pause, yawn, bang-bang, pause, snore, bang-bang. Reload, second verse same as the first. You were trying to shoot each target really fast twice, but were in no hurry moving your gun from one target to the next. On a drill like this, any time not spent shooting is wasted. This time, don't try to necessarily be so fast on each target, but try to have your split times be the exact same as your transitions. It should sound like bang-bangbangbangbangbang, and to anyone listening should sound like you're shooting six rounds into the same target, with no pauses. Trying to keep a constant cadence will force you to move the gun to the next target quicker. You see what I'm saying? Let's try it."

He ran me again, and I shot each target a little slower, but pushed the gun faster between targets. "Seven point one nine," he told me, turning the timer so I could see the readout. He squinted at the targets. "A full second faster. And your hits are about the same."

"It felt like I was shooting slower," I said, surprised.

"You were. But you didn't waste time moving your gun from target to target, so it ended up being faster overall."

Not quite fifteen minutes later I was loading magazines inside the barn when a cruiser from the Oakland County Sheriff's Department came rolling down the gravel driveway. "Boys!" I called out.

Splits and Transitions

We were waiting patiently when the deputy exited his car. "Afternoon, deputy. How can we help you?"

He gave me a dirty look. His eyes roamed over the pistols on our hips. "You can stop shooting," he told us. "We've gotten ten calls."

All of us looked to the west at the nearby subdivision. A few roofs were visible.

"They can suck it," Ron said warmly. "They moved in next to us." I rolled my eyes as the deputy bristled.

"Disturbing the peace, noise ordinance violations...you want me to go on?" the deputy said sharply.

I frowned but kept my mouth shut. I actually wasn't sure of the legality of what we'd been doing. I'd assumed it was legal, but given the way my month had been going...

"Officer, can I help you? I'm the property owner," we all heard, and turned to see George Kelly walking down from the house.

"Complaints called in about the shooting, sir, you're going to have to shut it down."

George had a smile on his face and kept it there as he walked up to the deputy. He was a few inches shorter than the uniformed man, but six inches wider and at least a hundred pounds heavier, most of that muscle. Even in his fifties he was intimidating as hell. "Well, I'm sorry you had to run all the way out here for that," George said apologetically. "Waste your time."

"It's not a waste of my time."

"Well, you're working hard," George said, smiling widely, although if you looked close you could see the smile didn't reach his eyes. "I'm just disappointed in the dispatcher, not telling whoever called that we have the legal right to be out here shooting. It was a waste of your time even giving you the call." He shrugged his huge shoulders.

"But I suppose you have to come out, make sure we're not doing anything illegal."

"You can't be shooting out here. There are houses right there," the deputy said, pointing.

George kept smiling. "Son, I've lived here for twenty-two years. For all that entire time, we've been shooting out here. Legally. It's not a violation of any state, county, or township ordinance or law, unless somebody passed one in the last month or so that I have not been made aware of. Is that the case?" He peered up at the deputy.

The deputy tried to regain control of the situation. "Sir, twenty-two years ago, those houses were not there."

"And neither were those berms I pushed up a couple years ago. Would you like to inspect them? Six feet high, which is considered the standard."

"You're welcome to join us," I told the young deputy, who looked about thirty. He shot me a dirty look.

"Probably won't be much more than another hour," Jerry told him, trying to be helpful.

"You need to shut it down now," he told us, tired of the dance.

"Not going to happen," George said, firmly but politely.

I smiled and backed up two feet. Then I slowly pulled out my cell phone, making sure my movements in no way looked like I was going for my gun.

"It's my day off," I heard in my ear.

"Mine too," I told Scott Copley. "But seeing as we just patched things up I'm hoping I can impose on you for a professional favor."

"Oh God, what now?"

"I'm at George Kelly's place. We've been doing a little shooting. Apparently some of the new neighbors don't like the noise. I've got a…" I looked over at his nameplate. "Deputy Twombly out here, telling us to shut it down."

"And of course those teenage psychos have no interest in doing that."

"Scott…" I took a breath. "George Kelly is here as well, politely talking to your man, but they seem unable to come to an agreement."

"He's back from…."

"From wherever he was." Scott knew what George did for a living.

"Fine, fine, hold on."

Ten seconds later the deputy held a hand up as his radio squawked, and backed away from George to answer a call. He put the speaker up to his ear, then changed the channel on his prep radio, backed up to his car, and had a brief conversation with someone on the other end. It ended with him saying, "Yes, sir."

He frowned at us in general, then me in particular as he knew I'd made the call. "You gentlemen have a nice day," he ultimately said, before getting back in his car and backing up the driveway fast enough to throw gravel.

"Sweet!" Jerry said. "Let's get back at it."

I traded a look with George. "This has not been as relaxing as I'd hoped," I announced.

An hour later I was sitting in my car, the A/C going full blast, but still I was sweating. I'd put the call off a day longer than I should have, but I really didn't want to make it. Afraid of what I'd learn. But being an adult is doing the things you have to, whether or not you like it. My dad had told me that repeatedly while growing up. I hadn't liked the sound of it then, either.

"This is Dr. Harmon," I heard in my ear. She sounded a bit out of breath.

"Yeah, doc, I'm calling about a puppy you guys picked up on the west side a couple days ago. Husky mix, from the look of it. Gray/white, fluffy. It had been shot in the head." I could hear barking in the background.

"And who are you?"

"I'm the guy who called it in."

"It was the DPD who called us."

I sighed, and fought against the flashbacks of that day. "I'm the one who called them. I…grabbed the guys who shot it."

"And scared the shit out of them, from what I heard," she said briskly. Maybe…cheerfully?

"Perhaps," I admitted. "I lost a dog, not too long ago, and it…" I wasn't sure why I was telling her personal details, and shut myself down. "Anyway, did you end up having to put him down?"

"Her," she told me. "And no."

I blinked. "No?" The dog had been shot in the head. She must have guessed what I was thinking.

"They shot her in the back of the head. But the bullet went in at an angle, and instead of entering the skull it just skimmed around the side, between the skull and the dermis, and exited above her left eye. Lot of blood loss, hairline fracture of the skull, probable concussion, but I don't think there's going to be any permanent damage."

"Seriously?" A weight I hadn't known was there lifted from my heart. And I think she could hear it in my voice. She laughed.

"Yeah. She was lucky. She's going to take a while to recover. But after that…if you know anybody who wants a puppy, we're at max capacity down here. I'd hate for her to have gone through all this, just for us to have to put her down again, you know?"

"Absolutely. I'll ask around. How long do I have?"

"Two weeks, give or take. What's your name?"

"John. John Phault."

"I'm Heather. Maybe you could come down and see her sometime."

I realized there was a huge smile across my face. "I'd like that."

Chapter Twelve

It had been five days, and there'd been no sign of Sullivan or his blue Mustang. I hadn't been on Kerrie Edwards every time she left her house for work or school, she didn't have that kind of money and I didn't have that much free time, no matter how guilty I felt for losing him…twice…but I still hated to leave something undone. I'd had Jerry take her from work to school the day before, and Mike take her to and from work the day before that, mostly because the surveillance I'd had scheduled for him was pulled by the client at the last minute and I wanted to give him something to do.

I had a late afternoon meeting with my lawyer about the divorce which left me both angry and nauseous. Afterward I didn't feel like eating dinner, so I hit the gym and worked out for two hours. Getting into the car, shaky because I'd nearly killed myself in an attempt to stop my brain from constantly going over the 'what ifs', I checked my watch, then decided to make a run by Kerrie Edwards' house.

The sun had been down for a while. One thing I hadn't

noticed before as I turned onto her street—there were no streetlights. The ribbon of blacktop was a shadowy corridor running straight and narrow before me. The houses were dark shapes set back from the road with here and there lights and illuminated windows.

I paused my vehicle in front of the house and rolled my window down. The evening was quiet. The porch light was on, and there was a light in the front room. No vehicles in the driveway, and no vehicles parked anywhere on the street at all. After thirty seconds I pulled my foot off the brake and the SUV started to roll forward. As the far side of the house came into view I saw another light on in the kitchen—I'd been inside the house once, and had a rough recollection of the floor plan.

I drove to the end of the block and circled around the street paralleling it to the south, Banmoor Drive, but there was no sign of Sullivan or his Mustang there either. Which was a good thing, objectively, but by not locating him the threat continued. The lots were so deep I could barely catch a glimpse of Edwards' house through the trees during the day—at night I wasn't even sure if I was in the right spot as I squinted between the houses on Banmoor.

Back at my apartment I parked out front and grabbed the debris that had started to accumulate in the back seat of the Tahoe, along with my gym bag, and headed inside. I threw the assembled trash onto the kitchen table along with my gym bag and hit the shower, first retrieving my SIG out of the bag and bringing it with me into the bathroom. I set it on the back of the toilet tank where it was easily accessible from the shower stall.

Talk to me about 'irrational paranoia' after you've had the Assistant Deputy Director for Operations of the CIA, running a completely off-the-books operation, send entire teams of covert operatives to kidnap and/or kill you and your friends—with some success, I might add.

Dressed in a t-shirt and shorts I headed back into the kitchen to get a snack and was confronted by the pile of trash on the table, which I'd forgotten about. I set the SIG down and grabbed two handfuls of fast-food bags and newspapers and threw them in the trash. And there, at the top of the heap, was the week-old copy of the Detroit News with the photo of Bernard Mitton's mistress, Esther Parnell, and her attorney.

I stared at it. Something about the photo was still bothering me. Frowning, I fished the newspaper out of the trash, then sat down in front of my computer, which was shoved into a corner. What I hadn't left at the house or stuck in a storage unit was still enough to clutter the apartment.

Before I dived into the quicksand that was the internet at large I checked the websites of the local newspapers and TV stations. Some of them didn't have much of an online presence, and most of the rest didn't keep their websites as up-to-date as I would have liked (the websites were free, and they wanted you to buy the newspaper, after all), but luckily the Mitton story was old news by that point.

I found, and skimmed, a number of stories, but they didn't tell me anything I didn't already know. There were more photos of Mitton and his wife, and then the video I'd already seen of the two of them at a black-tie charity event several years earlier.

Esther Parnell, the mistress, was of more interest to me, but there wasn't a whole lot of information about her. She was described as a "forty-two-year-old former office manager", which was as non-descriptive a description as you could hope for. She was a pretty, slender redhead; that I could see with my own eyes from the photos taken at the press conference where she'd done nothing other than stand behind her lawyer while he'd read a statement.

Purely by accident I virtually stumbled across a video of the entire six-minute press conference. It started with Parnell and her lawyer stepping up to a little podium adorned with a few microphones. I wasn't sure where they were but guessed it was outside his offices. She stood behind him, looking sad, as he told the world about her love for Bernard Mitton and their history together. When he was finished the assembled reporters shouted questions at him.

He smiled condescendingly, and when they quieted down enough to hear him, told them that neither he nor his client would be answering any questions, and that they looked forward to settling the matter of Mitton's estate as quickly and with as little drama as possible.

"I bet," I muttered, considering how many millions she was reportedly due.

Then the lawyer turned and took her elbow, and they walked away from the podium, up two steps, fifteen feet down a sidewalk, and through the front doors of an office building. Perhaps in Birmingham, if I had to guess. But the location isn't what made me sit up and rewind the video to the beginning of the statement.

I leaned close, studying the grieving mistress' face during the lawyer's speech, and her few expressions. Then I watched her very carefully at the end of the video, as she walked into the building. I watched that part several times.

"Am I crazy?" I muttered.

It only took me a minute to track down that video of Mitton and his wife at the black-tie event. I watched the two of them walk across the marble floor of whichever fancy downtown building they were in. I re-watched the video three times, then watched the mistress walking away three times. I went back and forth between the videos, then looked down at the newspaper at my elbow. There, on the front page, was the photo from the press conference, Esther Parnell staring straight ahead.

I stuck my thumb over the top of her head, hiding her red hair, and tried to imagine, instead, blonde hair. I looked from the photo under my thumb to the image of the late Mrs. Mitton on my computer monitor, and back to the newspaper.

"Son of a bitch," I said finally, slumping back into the chair, not sure if I should be angry or impressed. "She Chinatowned me."

Chapter Thirteen

"Detective George"

He sounded as irritated as I felt after getting bounced around the Detroit Police Department phone system for twenty minutes. "Are you the lead dick in the Bernard Mitton homicide?" I asked him.

"I'm not lead, but I'm working it. Can I help you?" He tempered his irritation slightly and added a touch of professionalism, I'm guessing because I spoke proper English, and used a bit of cop lingo.

"My name is John Phault. I'm a private investigator, based out of Troy. I may have information pertinent to your investigation on Mitton."

"Hold on." I heard a grunt and a lot of rustling. "Okay. What kind of information?"

"I don't know that I can tell you yet. I don't want to violate client confidentiality and put my license in jeopardy. If it even applies. This is a bit weird." She had the right to expect some confidentiality, or would have if she hadn't lied about who she was. Still, I was hesitant to start throwing out accusations. Especially when I realized I had no proof. And wasn't 100% sure it hadn't been Gloria Mitton who'd hired me. Maybe only 97%. 96%.

He made quite an unflattering sound. "You're the one who called us, buddy. You want to call back when you're pretty sure you can do something other than waste my time?"

"Yeah, I know, kind of an asshole move. Look, last October. I was hired to work a case involving Mitton."

"Involving him how?"

"That's where it gets dicey, and where I want to be careful. Case like this, I know you're into the financials of everybody. I was paid cash. Ten grand up front, on October eighth, and another thousand and change on the nineteenth to settle up the bill. Surveillance. I suspect the person who hired me misrepresented their identity. If that's the case, they forfeit client confidentiality, but… Anyway, Mitton and his wife are both dead, murdered even, so I'm in fact legally obligated to help out if I think I can. I need to know if, on or before early October last year, ten grand in cash, or more, was withdrawn from any of their accounts to pay me. If you can find any evidence Mitton or anyone connected to him paid my fee. If you find that is the case, then I can't help you."

"And if it wasn't?"

"Then I've got a story you'll want to hear. John Phault." I spelled it for him. "Phault Investigations and Security."

He called me back not quite four hours later. "Unless there's another account hidden somewhere, that money didn't come from the Mittons. They hardly did anything in cash, and never in amounts that big. Most of the really rich don't. They like paper trails. Their accountants have accountants. Unless Mitton pulled it out of one of his companies on the sly, but the forensic accountants we've had look over the books haven't thrown up any red flags yet." He paused. "So what do you have to tell me?"

"Last fall I was hired by Gloria Mitton to do surveillance on her husband. Ostensibly to see if he had a mistress. Followed him every day for ten days straight. Twelve, sometimes eighteen hours a day."

"You catch him with Parnell?"

"No. And now I'm pretty sure it wasn't Gloria Mitton who hired me. It was Parnell, in a wig and falsies, pretending to be Mitton."

I was greeted with a long silence on his end. "No shit?" he said finally.

"No shit."

"Hold on, let me…" I heard rustling papers. He was looking at photos. "Yeah…yeah, I can see that. Wig and a fake rack? They've got similar bone structure."

"I had no reason to suspect she wasn't who she said she was. Took me this long to even get suspicious. I'm guessing I need to copy all my reports for you. Maybe the video too? We took some video of him going back and forth. You want me to come down there?"

"I'll come to you. How long do you need to put it all together?"

Detective John George, as he was listed on his card, was younger than he sounded, maybe early thirties. Which explained why he wasn't lead detective on a case this big, he didn't have the experience or the seniority. His suit looked a little wrinkled, and he smelled of stale cigarettes.

We shook hands, and he sat down in front of my desk. I handed him the thick stack of reports—paper copies, as well as digital copies on CD. It included all the video we'd taken—she'd asked that we take video of Mitton's activities to document our work, even if he wasn't doing anything 'suspicious'. As client requests went, it wasn't unusual.

I'd gone over the entire file the night before, half to refresh my memory, half to see if I'd missed anything, now that I had a different perspective on the case. Nothing popped out at me. I hadn't watched the video yet—there were hours of it.

I gestured at the folder in his hands. "You can't fault Mitton for being lazy. Out of the house every day by seven-thirty. Did all his driving himself. He's got his personal office, which he visited every day, and satellite offices at two of the businesses he owns, and every two or three days for an hour or two he'd pop into a law firm that he seems to have on retainer. Probably putting all of the partners' kids through expensive colleges. Then, more often than not, in the evenings he would have some sort of event—party at his house, charity event downtown, DSO, DIA, high-brow stuff at the Fisher Theatre, big society dinner in Greektown or Birmingham or somewhere else they have valets and a dress code. Honestly I don't know how he found the time for a mistress, much less the energy, at his age."

"I hear Viagra's a hell of a drug. Was he out on his own enough to hook up with one?"

"Easily. He met his wife for lunch once at Fox & Hounds—"

"That the one on Woodward?"

"Yeah. Bloomfield Hills, about a mile from his house. But other than that, he never saw her during the day when he was working. He took a Sunday off, all he did was golf, and one Thursday he didn't seem to go anywhere. He was out with her just about every evening." I thought back to the surveillance reports I'd read the night before. "At least half the time he finished the work day at his corporate office. Twentieth floor of that office building on Woodward right at Campus Martius. 1001 Woodward. Fucking nightmare trying to follow him out of there, there's nowhere to park. Had to have two, three guys on him when he was downtown between the traffic and the one-way streets." I stopped, and opened and closed my mouth a few times. "He was killed right down there, wasn't he?"

George nodded. "Four blocks from his office building. Griswold and Clifford. He picked up his wife at home, then went out to eat on the riverfront, and were driving up to the Fisher Theatre to go see Le Miz." He peered at me. "You really think it was the mistress who hired you?"

"Pretty damn sure. They walk different. I had to watch videos of both of them, and it's been over six months, but still. With a wig and a stuffed bra or whatever she had in there she looked close enough to fool anyone who doesn't actually know Gloria Mitton, but the walk is definitely different. Not that I can prove it, but...."

"So why do you think she hired you to follow him?"

I blew out a mouthful of air. I'd asked myself the same question. "I have no idea. Could be completely innocent. Maybe she was worried he was seeing somebody else on the side other than her. But I know what I gave her." I pointed at the stack of reports in his hand. "A comprehensive record of his movements for ten days straight. The military and intelligence crowd would call that a target workup. You have any evidence this wasn't a totally random crime?"

He gave me a look. "Not until now. "

I gestured at the files in his hand. "That's still not evidence. Surveillance report that's now eight months old, and a scribbled signature two handwriting analysts couldn't agree on. Me thinking, maybe, most likely, that it wasn't the wife. But none of my guys saw her, just me. The phone number she provided is disconnected. I called it yesterday. Probably a burner."

"It's another angle to work. All that money she'd be coming into, that's a huge motive." He got a thoughtful look on his face, probably thinking the same thing as me—that the mistress had decided to take out Mitton while he was still infatuated with her, before something happened which soured the relationship and caused him to move on to another other woman, and yank her out of the will.

"You ever on the job?" he asked me.

"Federal. In my youth. Has she been cooperative?"

"Can't talk about an active case," he said with a shrug. "If I've got questions, need to talk to you or your guys who worked it?"

"Call me anytime, I'll set it up."

We stood and shook hands. He paused at the doorway, then turned and looked at me. "Not sure if I've ever heard her speak more than two words put together. Maybe she's just sad, in mourning. Her lawyer, on the other hand, likes to hear himself talk. Not that he ever says anything worth listening to."

"These people love their lawyers. Maybe she's just being very careful."

He gave me a look. "The rich usually are, when it comes to money. Big stacks of money."

"She's not rich yet."

"She will be, unless we can tie her to this."

"You think her lawyer will actually let her talk to you?"

He laughed, gave me a wave, and headed out.

Chapter Fourteen

I dropped by the house to pick up a few things I needed, and the alarming height of the grass in the front yard made me realize I'd forgotten to call a lawn service to take care of the place. Like I'd promised my wife I would. Two weeks earlier.

Which was how I found myself wrestling a push mower around the yard in near-ninety-degree heat for close to an hour, until the sweat was dripping off me. I put the lawn mower away in the garage, and stood in the shade looking out at the neighborhood. Middle, maybe upper-middle class street depending on where you drew the line, nicely maintained houses, landscaped yards, newer cars tucked away in attached garages. Those houses filled with hard-working Americans who lived boring, ordinary lives and raised normal children.

God how I envied them.

When I stepped out of the garage Dorian was in his front yard next door. Obviously waiting to talk to me.

"John! Glad you took care of that, it was getting a little long. Ummm…"

"Yeah?"

"Is the house…vacant? Haven't seen you guys in quite a while." He seemed tied up in knots trying to choose his words. Don't want to offend anyone.

"We've both moved out. Too many bad memories. Probably going to sell it pretty soon, so you'll be getting some new neighbors."

"Oh. Ummm." He looked up and down the street. "Are you…?"

"Am I what?"

He made a face and took a breath. "Are you in trouble with the police? I mean, there was a triple murder, right? The police won't really tell us anything, and then you guys were just…gone." He looked at me. "I thought you were in jail. I mean, I don't know that you did anything wrong, but—"

"Only one guy got shot in the house, and Kelly shot him," I said flatly. "After he shot Oscar."

His face paled at that. "Yeah, man, sorry about your dog. That's just crazy. But you're…."

"Nobody's in jail. Not me, not Kelly. It was justified. Everything. It just took a bit of time to get everything straightened out."

"And when you decide to sell the house…" He had a pained expression on his face.

"From what I've been told, state law requires you disclose if there's ever been a death inside. So my realtor will take care of that, you don't have to worry about it."

He chewed at his lip. "Right, right. And there's…. the guy who….?"

"What?"

He huffed a sigh at me, and found some suburbanite semblance of testicular fortitude. "Nobody in the neighborhood knows what the fuck happened, John. You say just one guy got shot in the house, but it was a triple murder, there were two more bodies over on Brewster. Should we be worried? Are we in danger? Police won't give us any information, and it all just disappeared from the news, almost overnight."

I understood his concern. "No. This was not a random crime. And what it was, that's over now. And we're moving. I hope whoever buys the house is boring and ordinary and a better neighbor than I was."

"Yeah. Great, thanks. Where are you moving?"

I shrugged. "I have no idea."

"Have you guys looked at any houses yet? My sister-in-law's a realtor."

"We're not together anymore," I said with a sigh.

That got him blinking. "Oh. Uh, I—"

My cell phone ringing saved him from any further embarrassment. "Excuse me," I said, and he was grateful for the excuse to back out of the conversation. It was Kerrie Edwards. I moved into the shade of the garage.

"He's here, I think. At work. In the parking lot."

I checked my watch. "Were you about to leave?" It wasn't quite four.

"No. I was coming back from the bathroom and went down a hall to look out the window for him, for his car, and I think I can see the back end of his car at the end of the lot. Are you here?"

"No, I'm nowhere near. You should have the phone number for the police department there. Call them, tell them you've got a stalker, you think he's in the lot, and that the last time you saw him he had stolen plates on his car.

That should get them moving. But don't leave the building if he's still there. Call the cops right now. Call me after, let me know what happened. And if you need me to come over there after work, follow you home, I can, although it might be closer to six."

"Okay." She sounded scared. I didn't blame her.

She called me back almost forty minutes later when I was on I-75 heading into Detroit. "I think it was him. He took off when they showed up, two cars, and he lost them. They came back and talked to me, after. Apparently he drove sort of crazy."

"More likely they probably have a departmental policy about pursuits." Still, it made me feel better about losing him.

"What do you mean?"

"Every time you go lights and siren, you risk lives, and that goes twice as much if you're chasing someone. A lot of departments only authorize pursuits if it's for a major, violent crime. Murder, bank robbery, the like. Stolen license plate and possible stalking doesn't rise to the level."

"Well that's just shitty," she said, angry. It made me smile. Anger was good. Anger was better than fear. Fear froze you. Anger got you moving.

"I can't see him returning to your office tonight. What you should do, though, tonight or soon, is head back to the Troy PD. Update the information you've given them. There have been two pursuits now, one involving the police. It should get them increasing the number of spot-checks of your mom's house. Do you have a report or incident number from the thing today?"

"Yeah."

"Give that to Troy, as well as the license plate that was on the Mustang when I chased him. Did he still have it on the car today?"

"I don't think they got close enough to see."

"Hmm. Well, unless something changes I should be able to follow you into work tomorrow morning."

"Thank you." She sounded like she was ready to cry. "This is crazy. I mean…it's just insane."

"We'll figure it out," I assured her.

Ten minutes later I was waiting patiently in a lobby. A noisy lobby. A stout middleaged woman was leading a large lab around on a leash, letting the kids there pet the dog. The dog was wearing a large vest, with the words EMOTIONAL SUPPORT ANIMAL embroidered on both sides.

"Is that a seeing eye dog?" I asked her. Leader Dogs for the Blind had their headquarters and training facility in Rochester. The dogs who could complete that training were the Green Berets of the dog world. The washouts still made great pets.

"No," she told me. "He's an emotional support animal."

I stared at her for a few seconds. "Of course he is," I finally said, a bit confused. "He's a dog. That's what dogs are. But is he actually trained to do anything?"

She was giving me a dirty look when a very short pretty woman in scrubs came out a door. She ran her eyes around the lobby, then headed my way. "Mr. Phault?"

"John, please. Doctor Harmon?"

"If you're John, I'm Heather," she said, and we shook hands. "Come on, follow me."

She moved quick, and even with her short legs I nearly

had to jog to keep up. After several twists and turns she led me into a small room lined with cages. "This is our medical ward," she said to me with a smile. She walked halfway down and then nodded at the cage on the left. I moved up beside her and stifled a laugh.

"Oh, buddy, I feel your pain," I said to the puppy. Half her head was covered by a bandage, and most of the rest was shaved. There was a cone around her neck.

"Had a cone around your head, have you?" the vet asked me with a smile.

"Probably wouldn't have been a bad idea. Especially in college." I smiled and gestured at the fuzzy puppy, who was maybe twenty pounds. "No, I've had a concussion. And been shot, but not in the head."

Harmon looked up at me, intrigued. Her wavy brown hair framed her face nicely, and she had quite a few curves under her scrubs. She opened her mouth, closed it, then said, "She's sedated right now, that's why she looks a little loopy. You find anybody who'd be willing to adopt her?"

I stared at the dog, who was half-asleep and not really focusing on anything. "Not yet."

"Well, we've got some time. And I won't do anything without calling you first." Out of the corner of my eye I saw her looking me up and down. She was tiny, and couldn't have been much more than five feet tall. I wasn't quite six-two, and after hitting the weights even harder than usual for the past few months was pushing two-twenty, so there was quite a size difference. "What do you do for a living?"

"Private investigator. I was down in that neighborhood on a case."

She didn't say anything, and after a bit I looked down at her. She was smiling at me. "Lucky for her," she said finally.

Chapter Fifteen

It wasn't as much video as I expected, or remembered. Even though my guys were given instructions to obtain video of Mitton whenever they could, most of the time when he wasn't home he was driving or inside a building. He wasn't prone to long walks around the neighborhood. Even when we did get lucky—like when I was seated near his table on the patio of a restaurant and obtained video of him using a hidden camera—I could fast forward through that seventy-three minutes of consecutive footage because most of it was just he and his wife talking and they were out of audio range.

I'd watched several hours of video the night before, then after following Kerrie Edwards to work—without incident or a sign of Sullivan—I returned to my office and viewed the remainder of the video. I didn't see anything that caught my attention or drew my eye. Nothing unusual, unexpected, or out of place. I hadn't expected to, but it still bothered me.

If Parnell was Mitton's only side-piece, to use a term my

young friends seemed fond of, she knew Mitton was under surveillance those ten days because she was paying for it. We'd seen no sign of her, wig or not, so she was staying away from him for the duration. I wonder where he thought she was, or what she was doing. At that thought I grabbed my phone.

"George."

"Detective. John Phault. I know you can't comment on an active investigation...but I guess I'm still asking you to comment on an active investigation."

He snorted. "Since you're so up to speed you could just say 'No comment' for me."

"I'm just reviewing the video we obtained of Mitton. Again. Probably going to re-read the reports a third time. I haven't seen anything that jumps out at me, and I'm just trying to figure out her game. Where he thought she was those ten days we were following him. Because she was nowhere to be seen."

I heard rustling papers. "According to you, she—or some woman as yet to be identified, but who claimed to be Gloria Mitton—first contacted you October fifth. Met you on October eighth, paid you a cash deposit, and you began ten days straight of surveillance the next day. Ran it through to the eighteenth. She met you again on the nineteenth to settle up the bill and collect the reports and video."

"Sounds about right."

"I'm not discussing an active case with you, understand, we're just verifying the information you provided. And I didn't happen to mention Esther Parnell flew down to Florida October ninth. Visiting her sister. She returned the eighteenth." He paused. "If there was anything that could unequivocally convince me it was her who came to see you dressed like the wife, it's the fact that she happened to be a thousand miles away the exact entire time you were following Mitton. It's too neat. No such thing as a coincidence. Maybe she was just worried about him trading her in for a younger other woman, but still. As for the time of the murder, she has a solid alibi."

"Doesn't mean she didn't pay someone to do it."

"Really? Wow, I hadn't thought of that. I should call you more often, get some of those expert tips."

I snorted. "You talk to her about this yet?"

"She and her lawyer are coming in tomorrow morning, to answer 'a few more questions'."

"Should be interesting. If I come across anything else I'll give you a call."

"That would be appreciated."

For the next two-plus hours I re-read all the surveillance reports. There was nothing there I hadn't seen before. I'd already talked to Jerry and Mike, asked them if they'd seen anything that somehow hadn't made it in to the reports, for whatever reason.

Nope.

I checked my watch. Jerry and Mike were out on a surveillance. There was nothing more for me to do in the office, so I headed out, forwarding the office phone to my cell and locking the door behind me.

Bernard Mitton and his wife lived—had lived—in Bloomfield Hills, a wealthy enclave split in two by Woodward Avenue several miles south of Pontiac, about ten miles north of the city limits of Detroit. I was pretty sure Elmore Leonard, the famous writer who most recently had seen big success with Hollywood adaptations of a few of his novels into the movies *Get Shorty*, *Jackie Brown*, and *Out of Sight*, lived in the area. A lot of local movers and shakers lived in the area, it was as upscale a neighborhood as there was in the Detroit area.

Their street, Orchard Ridge, was like many in the city—narrow, winding, tree-lined, and a nightmare if you were trying to perform a surveillance. Nobody parked on the street. Well, almost nobody—I lucked out. One of the older houses a quarter mile down Orchard Ridge had been demolished and a crew was building a replacement on the big lot. I parked behind the row of personal vehicles belonging to the work crew—mostly full-size pickups, so my Tahoe fit right in—and when the supervisor came wandering over a few hours later I explained the situation and offered to buy him and his guys lunch every day I was there.

Subs, pizza, and fried chicken for lunch, for free? Those guys loved me, and were sorry to see me go. Not that I sat there for very long, usually, Mitton was out and about every day but the one Sunday we worked him, and one Thursday, for whatever reason.

The houses were big, barely visible from the road if at all. We couldn't actually sit where we could see the house, as we would have been spotted immediately by anyone leaving the house, and the client (who I'd thought at the time was Mrs. Mitton) wasn't concerned with who might be visiting him at their home, only what he was doing while he was away from home. I always had to have two guys work the case, one vehicle at either end of the street to pick up the car as it left. Or one at the end of the street and me hidden in plain sight at the construction site. Still, I had to call in to the Bloomfield Hills PD every day, and half the time they sent out a car anyway just to check us out, make sure I—we—were who I said we were. They honestly didn't have much else to do.

Mitton's house was big and hulking, with a circular driveway and an attached four-car garage on a two-acre lot. There were no cars visible when I drove by, and no activity. Pretty much what I was expecting, but the case was bothering me. Bothering me enough that I drove down to Detroit to look at the intersection where Mitton and his wife had been killed. It was getting near to rush hour, but luckily I was heading in the opposite direction of traffic, so it took me less than forty-five minutes. I took Woodward southeast to I-696 east to southbound I-75. Into the city I-75 split off to the west, and I took the I-375 stub and got off on westbound Jefferson. From there it was barely half a mile to the scene of the crime.

Northbound Griswold dead-ended at Clifford a short block from Woodward in the business district of downtown Detroit. There was a stop sign at the intersection, but no light. Buildings towered around on all sides—one parking garage, a few office buildings with retail businesses on the ground floor, and a few apartment buildings.

I pulled to the curb and got out. Looked around, craning my neck up. There were hundreds, maybe thousands of windows that looked down on the intersection, but that hour of night, how many people were looking out of them, much less down at the intersection? And how much could they see, if the street lights were even working? Someone important like Mitton, I knew the DPD would have officers knocking on every door of every business or apartment which overlooked the intersection, looking for somebody, anybody, who saw or heard anything. If they had, they were keeping it away from the media. I could see a few security cameras mounted on the buildings along Clifford, but what they showed of the crime, if anything, the police were also keeping to themselves.

Cars drove by me regularly, pausing at the stop sign and turning right or left. While we were on him, Mitton twice, or maybe three times, had taken Griswold as the back way out of his office building. Up to this corner, and turned right, then hooked an immediate left onto Woodward. His actual route wasn't detailed in our reports, just where he landed, and when, but…but….

A sour taste in my mouth, I drove over to Lafayette Coney Island, just a quarter mile away. I got two with everything, which in Detroit means two dogs with chili, onions, and mustard. I fielded calls from Jerry and Mike as they detailed the events of the day's surveillance. We talked about the cases I had scheduled them on for the rest of the week. Then I headed up to Troy.

My cell phone rang as I was pulling up in front of the gym. I didn't recognize the number. "John Phault."

"John? Hi. It's Heather. From the Humane Society?"

"Oh yeah, hi. Is everything okay with the puppy?"

"She's doing just fine. Healing nicely. That's not why I called, actually. I was wondering if you wanted to go out to eat some time. Dinner." Not one bit of hesitation. I knew I liked her. She just went for it.

"I'm…" I struggled for the right words. "Amazingly flattered, actually," I told her. "Seriously, you have no idea. However," since she charged in so bravely, with no hesitation, she deserved no less from me, "I'm in the middle of a rather messy divorce. I'm not sure how enjoyable my company might be. I mean, normally I'm amazing, but…." Was I not wearing a wedding ring when I met her? I kept meaning to take it off, but couldn't bring myself to do it. I looked at my left hand. No, there it was. Maybe she preferred married guys, as there was no chance of something serious developing.

"I saw the ring," she admitted, "but you didn't have a 'happily married' vibe. I'm pretty good at reading people, and you seemed…headed for an exit. Is there a chance at reconciliation?"

"Wow, you just dive right the hell in, don't you?"

"Life's too short. I'd rather regret the things I did than didn't do."

I took a deep breath and let it out. "No. Much as I would like…we're done. My brain knows it, I'm just waiting for my heart to catch up. Then, I suppose, the ring'll come off. Right now it's just inertia keeping it there." I kept staring at it, wrapped around my finger. When I took if off, there was a deep groove in my flesh. Jesus, how long had it been since I'd been on a date? A decade, maybe more.

"Do you think you can get through a meal without crying or talking incessantly about your wife?"

I smiled. "I'm pretty sure I could muddle through. Who doesn't like a challenge? As long as you're willing to grade on a curve."

"So that's a yes?"

"I suppose it is."

Chapter Sixteen

I was doing a solo work comp surveillance just off Seven Mile Road, east of Gratiot. Ninety percent of PI work is insurance related. Ninety percent of insurance work involves workers compensation claims, and ninety percent of that is surveillance. All of which meant I spend a lot of time sitting in bad neighborhoods, waiting for something to happen, intermittently relieving myself in a bottle and listening to talk radio. And thinking about the mechanics of crime and urban decay. For example:

The "bad" areas of Detroit, versus the "good" areas of Detroit:

Some areas have a higher crime rate, that's true, but just how safe you might be in any particular neighborhood has much more to do with the time of day than anything else. At six a.m. in the city of Detroit, or in any city, the crime rate is just about zero, because almost all the troublemakers are sleeping. The later it gets after, say, eleven a.m., the greater likelihood you're going to have some problems.

My current surveillance assignment was in one of the

highest crime rate areas of the city, but at eight a.m. nobody was awake. In the two hours I'd been sitting in my Tahoe I'd seen a grand total of one resident drive off, presumably to work. I'd seen more stray dogs than people. Admittedly, at least half the block was vacant land, there were more teeth in a homeless man's head than there were houses on the first block south of Seven Mile, but in the afternoon the area came alive. I wouldn't actually be able to do an effective surveillance in the area if I had to arrive in the afternoon. Every eye on the block, and there'd be a lot of people sitting on their porches by three or four p.m., would lock onto my strange vehicle if I pulled onto the street late in the day. Everyone would assume I was a cop as opposed to a PI, but the end result would be the same—the word would go out, and nobody would do anything hinky within sight of my vehicle. They'd wait for me to leave. Sometimes patiently, sometimes not. If you've never had carloads of gangbangers driving around the block repeatedly as they eye your vehicle, trying to decide who you were, and if you were a threat, I really recommend it as a way to get the heartrate up. Cardio without having to pay those expensive gym fees.

There was a spot of shade, and I'd parked in it, facing south, Seven Mile about fifty feet behind my rear bumper. To my left was a vacant lot empty of everything but two-foot-tall grass swaying in the occasional breeze and a mattress that was now a mottled brown color. To my right was a long single-story commercial building that at some point in its past had been a hand car wash. The building was crumbling, and showed smoke damage from a recent fire.

The claimant owned a red Chevy, and it was parked on the curb in front of the house at the far end of the block.

The client only wanted six hours done on this new case, so I was going to work it until noon and then break off if the claimant wasn't active. She was suffering from "bilateral epicondylitis", what regular people would call tennis elbow, in her case in both arms. The doctor she was seeing had given her physical restrictions which included no repetitive motions and no lifting over ten pounds.

The vast majority of work comp claimants I'd done surveillance on had legitimate injuries. I got called in when the claimant was unexpectedly delayed in returning to work. "Suspected malingerers", the English would call them. However, it wasn't that simple, at least when it came to my job, which on this case was observing and documenting the claimant's activity.

If you're out on a back injury claim, and the doctor tells you not to pick up anything heavier than (X) pounds, that's a doctor-imposed 'restriction'. If a PI gets film of you wrestling a bar-b-que grill down the back stairs of your house, it doesn't necessarily prove anything. Just because a doctor tells you not to do something doesn't mean you physically can't. Just because you were able to do it doesn't mean it didn't hurt like hell, either right then or the next morning. Or both.

Much more important are limitations. If a claimant, while speaking to a company doctor or a doctor at an Independent Medical Evaluation, says he or she simply can't do X, or Y, that is a limitation. A self-imposed one. And if a PI gets video of that claimant doing something they explicitly said they couldn't do, that's far more important, and useful. They've been caught in a lie.

Thanks in large part to the heavy union presence in the area (UAW, Teamsters, etc.) almost nobody in Michigan goes to jail for insurance fraud. If I was able to document a claimant doing something that violated their restrictions, the insurance company tended to use it as leverage against the claimant. Or try to use it, sometimes unsuccessfully. If I documented a claimant doing something that clearly violated their self-imposed limitations, the client would usually shut off their benefits immediately and tell the claimant to get back to work immediately or they'd be fired.

In many ways, the divorce work is more honest and less sleazy.

Insurance is a necessary evil—both necessary, and evil. In my experience, at least half of all insurance companies will try to deny half of all claims regardless of legitimacy, because paying out on claims isn't good for the bottom line. As a huge supporter of capitalism, the only thing that regularly makes me question my economic philosophy is dealing with insurance companies.

After two hours of nothing happening I was in my usual stupor, staring down the block at the claimant's car while letting my mind wander. I wondered what had happened during the meeting between Detective George and Ms. Parnell and her lawyer, but resisted the urge to call him. I'd already stretched my luck, and he'd given me far more info than I'd expected, or that he should have. Then again, I'd given him what I suspected was his only good lead in the case so far, based on the few things he'd said, so maybe he'd been feeling generous. Either way, I wasn't going to get any more updates on the case, not from him. If any arrests were made, I'd learn about them the same way as everyone else in Detroit—the local news.

By late morning the sun had moved and I was no longer in the shade. It was very humid and the temperature had already climbed into the eighties, so I turned on my vehicle and ran the air conditioner. Ten minutes later I was counting down the minutes until I could break off the surveillance and head for the office when I caught movement in one of my mirrors, but then it was gone. I glanced over my shoulder, in my blind spot, and saw a hooker heading my way. Apparently she'd been drawn to the sound of my running engine.

She walked up and stood just outside my door. I had the window cracked half an inch, just to better hear neighborhood sounds. "Hey," she said with a smile that only showed one missing tooth. "You lookin' to party?" She was white, and skinny, and maybe thirty, wearing a flowered halter top over denim shorts. Crack or meth was her drug of choice, if I had to guess from her emaciated body.

I shook my head. "I'm working," I told her flatly. If you gave them any encouragement at all they would never leave.

"Aw, come on," she said. She moved up close and began rubbing herself against the door of my Tahoe. "Cops need love too," she told me. So she thought I was a cop and still propositioned me. Which should tell you all you need to know about that area of the city.

I glanced up the block, just to make sure my claimant hadn't gone anywhere, then back at her. "Go away," I told her.

"You sure?" she asked, making one last pitch, pulling up her halter top. She wasn't wearing anything underneath.

"I'm flattered, but no."

She tugged her top back down. "Asshole," she said perfunctorily, no heat behind the word. It was a reflex. She turned and headed back to Seven Mile and disappeared around the corner of the burned-out former car wash.

"Christ," I muttered, and checked my watch. Seventeen minutes left. Noon couldn't arrive soon enough.

Splits and Transitions

Seven hours later I was sitting in the Starbucks near my office, finishing up a report on my laptop. I was in one of my two preferred seats which put my back to a wall and gave me a view of both doors and the entire coffee shop, which wasn't very large.

Instead of doing the report as soon as I'd gotten back to the office I'd made a number of overdue phone calls, worked out for two hours, then followed Kerrie Edwards from her office building back home. There'd been no sign of Sullivan for a several days, which didn't sit well with either one of us. I didn't see him just ending his harassment and pursuit of her. Not without something major happening to dissuade him. The police arresting him might do the trick. Then again, it might not.

Something was bothering me, and my typing slowed, then finally stopped. I took a sip of coffee and used the movement to look around the Starbucks. There were a few people sitting at the tables, and two in line at the counter. It was still light enough outside I could see the cars in the parking lot, although their interiors were shadowed. I didn't actually see anyone or anything…but my spidey senses were tingling. It felt like I was being watched.

Frowning, I checked to either side, just to make sure my back was, in fact, to the wall, and that there was nobody sneaking up on me. Nobody in the place was paying me the slightest bit of attention, but I couldn't shake the feeling. Finally, after ten minutes of not typing a single word, I packed up my laptop and headed out to the Tahoe.

If anyone was following me I did everything I could first to spot them, and then to lose them—unexpected U-turns, speeding, driving much slower than the speed limit, making three right turns, every trick I knew to try and spot a tail. If anyone was behind me I never spotted them, but if they were there I lost them with a few shenanigans that got horns blaring.

I finished the reports at the apartment, SIG on the table next to the laptop, AR-15 leaning against the side of the couch. Then got a good night's sleep.

Chapter Seventeen

Mike was a decent report writer, but sometimes I had to translate his cop lingo and acronyms into English before sending his surveillance reports in to the adjusters, none of whom had prior law enforcement experience. With Jerry's reports, I sometimes had the opposite problem—an occasional lack of professionalism in choosing his adjectives. And adverbs. And nouns.

I spent the morning editing three reports and on the phone with a few clients, lining up some more work. Then I called Mike.

"Robinson's got a couple more subpoenas for us to deliver on that big accidental death case he's got brewing. Pick 'em up when you're done today, if it's not too late. Are you still a notary public?"

"Yeah, why?"

"I don't know. He was asking if you were a notary. Give him a call. I don't know if it's related to the subpoenas or something else."

"Gotcha."

When I looked up from my desk Bob Grinnand was standing in front of it, a small, almost shy smile on his face. He was in jeans and a plaid button-down over a white t-shirt.

"Well holy shit," I said.

He was shockingly skinny, at least for Bob. To anyone else he would have looked like an athletic young man in his mid-twenties. Considering he normally look like Thor, God of Thunder, it was a big step down. His hair was short, and his big jaw was clean-shaven.

I jumped up and came around the desk. "You breakable?" I asked.

His smile got a little wider. "No, I'm good."

I gave him a big hug, then stepped back and looked at him again. "You can't call first?"

He shrugged. "Still trying to keep a low profile." He sat down in the client's chair in front of the desk. I had talked to him half a dozen times over the past six months, but the last time I'd actually seen him was just after New Year's. He'd still been in a wheelchair from his injuries.

"You're skinny," I told him.

"You've bulked up."

I shrugged and sat back in my chair. "You look good," I told him. "You working out yet?"

"Not really. I'm running two or three slow miles and doing bodyweight exercises, push-ups, sit-ups, that kind of things, but not lifting actual weights yet."

"Well, you died," I pointed out. "Two or three times, whatever." They'd restarted his heart every time, but rebooting your hard drive can be quite a shock to the system, or so I imagine. And then there were the broken ribs, the punctured lung, the six gunshot wounds….

"Still, it's been six months," he complained.

"You want me to get out my violin?" I asked him. "I know a few sad songs."

He looked at me and smiled, but it was a sad smile, and the sadness had nothing to do with his injuries. I'd escaped the incident with just a broken arm and foot, both of which were long healed. Well, plus a concussion, some stitches, and a ruptured eardrum, but my worst injuries weren't physical. And both of us knew it. He shared my pain, he'd lost a fiancée to a grenade meant for him.

"Are you worried Iraq will be over before you get there?" Changing the subject worked for both of us.

He shook his head. "If it's not Iraq or Afghanistan it'll be somewhere else. There's always shitty people doing shitty things to each other."

"Job security," I told him.

He shrugged. "I don't think Iraq will be over any time soon. They still haven't found Saddam. Or his two asshole sons."

"Are you on leave? How long you in town for?"

"Just a few days," he told me, "see my parents and you chuckleheads. Jerry's working for you?" He cocked his head and I nodded.

"Ron once or twice too. Steve's in-process with the DEA, which should be interesting."

He snorted. "Yeah."

We both heard the front door of my office open. "In here!" I called out.

Bob looked at me and mouthed the word "Client?" I shrugged.

Two big guys I'd never seen before crowded through the doorway and looked back and forth between the two of us. The fact that I was the guy behind the desk probably clued them in on who I was, but I could see they weren't expecting me to have a guest.

"Hi, John Phault, can I help you?" I asked helpfully.

"Beat it, fuckface," the bigger one said to Bob out of the corner of his mouth, then they squared off at me, along the side of my desk, ignoring Bob. It seemed they assumed he'd take their advice.

"You need to stop talking shit about Esther Parnell," the smaller one said to me. He was still six feet tall, with a lot of muscle. Gym rats, from their builds. White guys, in their late twenties. I'd never seen them before.

"You don't know her, you've never met her, and we're here to make sure you know she doesn't appreciate you telling lies about her." Both of them huffed and puffed and flexed their fists. They made my office feel small.

Bob spread his hands in a 'what the hell' gesture. I just shook my head at him, dumbfounded.

"Is it me?" he asked. "It's got to be me." He looked up at the two big men from his chair, frowning.

"It is you," I told him. "Scott Copley once accused me of being loaded with a natural disaster chemical, but it's you who's the shit magnet. I haven't had one single incident since Maryland."

"Neither have I," he said defensively. It sounded as if I'd hurt his feelings.

Our two visitors seemed a little put out that we weren't taking them more seriously. It was simply a matter of experience. Bob had probably killed more people than they'd ever met, and I'd had one hell of a year as well, so them threatening me with a little bit of physical injury had far less of an effect than it would have on the normal person. Besides, they were empty-handed, I was armed, and I would have been willing to bet any amount of money that Bob was armed as well. Not that he really needed to be, I had no doubt that even in his current weakened condition he could kill all three of us with his bare hands without breaking a sweat.

The two men moved forward, crowding the two of us even more.

"Dudes," Bob said to caution them, shaking his head a little bit.

The man closest to him put his hand on Bob's shoulder, clamping it down. Quick as a snake Bob's right hand darted over, flicked up, and I heard the crunch of fingers breaking. Bob's foot shot out at nearly the same time, catching the other man between the legs, hitting him so hard there was daylight underneath his shoes. Briefly, but does that really matter? Unintelligible squeals spilled from both their mouths as they went down.

Before the second man even hit the floor I had my gun out and pointing at them. Muzzle of my SIG pressed against the groin-kicked writhing man's nose I checked him for weapons, and then the second man. Neither of them had guns, all I found was a folding knife on the man who now had what looked like two broken fingers. The bigger of the two, rocking back and forth on his side, clutching his midsection, puked noisily on my floor. Bob never even got out of the chair, he just sat there watching us.

I pulled their wallets out, then found their driver licenses. I reholstered my SIG, grabbed my digital camera off the shelf, and took several photos of their licenses. Then I put away the camera, drew my pistol again, and sat back down. I was in no hurry.

When both of the men had recovered from the pain enough to be able to focus on my words I told them, over the muzzle of my still-pointed gun, "I understand, this was business, not personal. I don't really have any hard feelings. You know who I am, and now I know who you are." I gestured at their wallets still sitting on my desk. "But, since this is business, if I see either of your two faces again I'm just naturally going to assume you're there to escalate the conflict. So I want to let you know ahead of time that if I do see either one of you ever again I am just going to shoot you in your faces. In fact, if anything you do in any way makes me feel threatened, there's a good chance I'll just come to your house in the middle of the night and shoot you in the back of the head. Just in case. Better safe than sorry, right?" My big smile seemed to be confusing them, as it was such a contrast to what I was saying.

I leaned down and tapped the muzzle of my SIG on the forehead of the closest man, then moved over and did the same to the second. They both stared up at me with wide eyes, perhaps because I seemed so calm about the whole thing. "Do we understand each other?" I asked them quietly. They both nodded.

I sat back down behind my desk, gun still in my hand, resting on my thigh. "Then get out," I told them. "Don't forget your wallets." They did as instructed, with some difficulty, and displaying no small amount of pain.

Bob watched them go from his chair, and when he heard the office door close he turned and looked at me. "I'm not even back on full active duty," he told me. "I've just been doing mission planning. I can't afford to get involved in anything like this." I gave him my best hurt expression.

"Is this anything interesting?" he asked.

"You wouldn't think so."

He just grunted, then peered at me the way he did. "How are you doing?"

Splits and Transitions

"You mean with the whole divorce because my wife hates me because she blames me for killing her baby? Our baby? And the dog?" I hadn't meant to snap at him.

He leaned back from me. "Well, I guess that answers that question."

I blew out air and popped my neck. "You want to get something to eat?"

Bob cocked his head, looked at the door of my office, then back at me.

"We'll give them some time to clear the building," I told him. "Their egos are already bruised enough."

He shrugged. "You do have some puke to clean up first."

I leaned over my desk and looked at the floor. Then sighed.

We went to The Alibi on Rochester Road in the north end of Troy, nearly to Rochester Hills. They had fabulous pizza and we ordered one with pepperoni, plus an antipasto salad. The salad came first and we'd devoured that, and were making great headway into the pizza, when Bob swallowed a big bite half-chewed and said, "Oh boy."

"What?" I asked, seeing the expression on his face, but he wasn't looking at me.

"Bob?" I heard. One of the other waitresses was standing beside our table. He just smiled up at her. She, on the other hand, looked confused. "I thought that was you," she said. "But, I mean, don't you…didn't you…?" She paused and tried to gather her thoughts. "Aren't you in trouble?" she asked. "I thought you were in jail."

"Jail?" I said.

She looked from me back to Bob. "For killing those

guys. It was all over the news. He cut his head off," she said distantly to me, as if she couldn't believe what she was saying.

"Cut someone's head off?" I said. "Wow. What movie was this?" Bob had a bemused expression on his face.

She looked back and forth between the two of us again. "No not a movie." She turned to stare at Bob. "You did it. You killed those people. I saw the video."

Bob just kept smiling at her, then finally said, "Don't you think if I killed a bunch of people I'd be in jail? It's good seeing you."

"Yeah, uh, yeah," she said, looking back and forth between the two of us. Looking very confused, she slowly walked away from the table.

"Man she's put on a lot of weight since high school," Bob said, taking a huge bite of pizza. We watched her talking to several other waitresses over by the kitchen. They kept glancing in our direction.

"I'm thinking we should make ourselves scarce," Bob finally said.

"I don't know," I told him with the smile, "I'd kind of like to see you explain things to the cops. Or try to."

"It's called a non-disclosure agreement because you're not supposed to disclose anything," he told me through his teeth in clipped syllables.

"Yeah, well, there is that."

I looked over at the huddled group of restaurant employees again. At the time of the incident in question, captured on video by a local news crew and broadcast everywhere until the NSA had done its best to erase its existence from the internet, Bob had been sporting a reddish beard and longer hair, as well as about twenty additional pounds of muscle. "I'm surprised she recognized you. High school?"

Bob followed my gaze. "I think we had sex," he said vaguely, chewing.

"You think?"

He shrugged his still-sizeable shoulders. "It's been five or six years. Lot's happened since then."

"Ain't that the truth," I told him. I dug some cash out of my pocket and threw more than enough on the table to cover the bill and provide a healthy tip. I nodded across the dining room. "Pretty sure that's the manager over there on the phone with the local constabulary. Perhaps discretion, valor, etcetera?"

"Yeah," he said, standing up, but he grabbed the last slice of pizza to take with.

We were in the car a block away when we saw the flashing lights behind us. The cop car swung into the restaurant parking lot at speed, and another wasn't far behind.

"I think I'm just going to head over to my parents' house," he told me with a sigh and a frown. "Stay the fuck out of the way of whatever you're involved in. I'm supposed to be keeping my head down. And off the news."

Chapter Eighteen

"Detective George."

He always sounded irritated. It put a smile on my face, hearing from a fellow traveler. "Detective, it's John Phault. PI, surveillance, Esther Parnell…"

"Yeah, yeah, I know who you are."

"You never call, you never write…"

"But I am about to hang up. Can I help you with anything?"

"Well, I just thought you might be interested in something that happened yesterday. I had two visitors to the office. Two young men. Very fit. Probably have their names Magic-Markered on their weight belts. They seemed very intent on making sure I stopped telling lies about Ms. Parnell. That I'd never met her, didn't know her, had never worked for her, etcetera. Only took a day after you talked to her about hiring me."

"No shit. They threaten you?"

"Not directly. More intimidation. It might have escalated if I'd let it, but I don't respond well to threats anymore."

"So what happened?"

"Sometimes, you're better off not knowing," I told him. "But, technically, I never laid a hand on them. We've agreed to live and let live."

He grunted, not quite sure what to make of my comment. "And they said they were working for her?"

"No, nothing so direct. Nothing actionable."

"Well, shit." He was silent for a while. "There's no way I could get a protective detail assigned, not up there. Have you talked to Troy?"

"I'm not asking for protection," I told him. "I can take care of myself. I'm not worried about a couple of amateurs. Bouncer types, more like, used to beating up drunks. I didn't even file a police report. I just thought you should have a heads-up. Them showing up to my office pretty much eliminates any doubt I had about her. Both her being the person who hired me, and why."

"It's still not evidence. Of anything."

"No, it is not. But that's your job," I said cheerfully. "Do you have any evidence tying her to it?"

"No comment," he grumbled.

"Have you developed any known associates of hers who might have been involved in the deed?"

"That's probably a no comment as well."

"Would you like the names and addresses of two of her associates? I'm not saying they're the two guys who came to visit me in my office, but I'm not *not* saying it."

There was a pause. "They gave you their names? And addresses?"

"They were carrying their driver's licenses. I took a picture. I can probably eFax it to you."

"Yeah," he said slowly. "Yeah. That'd be good."

"Bob's home one day and you've got him busting heads?" Jerry Phillips said in my ear, laughing. I heard Ron Kelly in the background and presumed they were at Ron's house. Then I heard shooting, confirming my suspicions.

"I wanted to blame him, but now I wonder if it's the two of us together. Like mixing two otherwise inert chemicals that when combined make a bomb."

"Bob's never been inert," Jerry reminded me. "And didn't you shoot someone when you were in the DEA? Years before you ever met us?"

I made a face, as I usually did when talking to Jerry. "Did you call for a reason?"

"Yeah. You've got guys showing up at the office, threatening you. You want some company, in case they come back?"

"Nah, I'm fine. Ask Bob, he'll tell you. Complete amateur hour."

"It's the amateurs that are dangerous. They're unpredictable. Seriously, they even made a movie about it. Spy movie, called The Amateur, based off a book. Late eighties. Pretty good."

"Don't worry about me. And threatening someone was the most productive thing I've done in weeks," I said, thinking about the elusive Michael Sullivan, and the last half dozen or so claimants on which I'd done surveillance, none of whom had gone anywhere or done anything. "Go have fun with Bob. Keep him out of trouble. You need tomorrow off?"

"Nah, I can work that case. He'll be hanging out with his parents tomorrow, then he's heading back."

"Where, Bragg?"

"Don't know, and I know better than to ask. He's doing mission prep for heavy hitters until he gets back in fighting shape, that's all he'll say. You stay safe, I don't want to have to go looking for a new job if you get killed."

It was late in the afternoon when the office phone rang. I picked it up and identified myself. "Uh, yeah, this is Ray," I heard.

"Hello Ray," I said pleasantly. "Ray who?"

"Um, Ray…the guy whose fingers you broke yesterday. In your office."

I blinked several times. This was a surprise. I remembered the first name Raymond from one of the driver licenses I'd had on my desk. "What can I do for you, Ray?" Technically Bob had been the one to break his fingers, but I'd had the gun in his face.

"Um, yeah." It was clear he was embarrassed. "Look, okay, no hard feelings you know, right? Like you said? Just business. Not personal. But you said if you saw my face again you'd shoot it. Shoot me. So I'm calling, instead of coming by. And I…" He sighed. "You took a knife off me. When I was there. A little folding knife?"

My chair creaked as I turned around. It was there on the shelf behind me. "Yes I did."

"My dad gave me that knife. When I was a kid. And, he's dead now…"

"Jesus, seriously?" It did look old. And had the shine of being carried in a pocket for years.

"Yeah."

Like I needed more guilt. I frowned at the knife. "When do you want to come by?"

"Ummm…"

"I won't shoot you," I assured him. "Unless you do something stupid, and then I will. But if all you really want to do is pick up the knife…."

"I'm kinda in the area now."

I was standing in the open doorway of my office, looking down the hallway, when he got off the elevator. His right hand was professionally splinted, and his left was empty. He was alone, and looked embarrassed. 'Hangdog' I think is an appropriate term.

Ray blinked at me as he got up close. I had at least an inch on him, and was just as muscled. "You're bigger than I thought," he said.

"I'm a lot shorter when I'm sitting down." I held up the knife. "I don't know if that's your regular gig, but you should find another line of work. It doesn't suit you," I told him. My PTSD-induced nightmares were not so frequent anymore, but they were a lot scarier than Ray.

"Yeah, well…"

I held out the knife, and he took it.

"I really appreciate—"

"You do a lot of work for Ms. Parnell?"

He shook his head. "I've done a few things with Buddy. That was the other guy. He got me the gig. We've bounced together at a few clubs."

Buddy was the bigger of the two. And a nickname, apparently, as the name on his license had been Richard. "How's he doing?"

"Nothing ruptured, so no permanent damage." He looked at me. "Pissed at you."

I hadn't touched the Buddy family jewels. I'd only lightly tapped him on the forehead. It had been with the muzzle of a handgun, but still. "He do a lot of work for Ms. Parnell?"

Ray shrugged. "I don't know."

"Do you know why she sent you to threaten me?"

"Just that you were harassing her. Stalking her."

"Is that what Buddy told you? Is that what she told Buddy?" He gave me a blank stare. Not a lot going on upstairs, but for a thug he seemed relatively pleasant. I decided to give him some helpful advice. "The cops are thinking she murdered her rich boyfriend. If you weren't involved in that, you might want to steer clear."

"I don't know anything about that. I don't even own a gun."

"What about Buddy? He own a gun?"

"Maybe."

"Would he use it, if he got paid?"

It took him quite a bit of thinking before he finally shrugged. "Go," I told him, jerking my head. I watched him walk all the way to the elevators, and stood there until he got on, before shutting my office door and getting back to work.

Chapter Nineteen

I'd never met Mark Ripley, but apparently a former client had recommended me to him, and he'd given my name to the two gentlemen who were currently in the dressing room behind me having a screaming fight. I checked my watch. They were due to go onstage in twenty minutes. There was a loud thunk and I felt it as something hit the door. Now they were throwing things. They'd been going at it for over an hour.

The stage manager of Ripley's Comedy Club had a strange look on his face as he tentatively walked down the narrow hallway toward me. I was stationed outside the door. I wasn't sure why a brother musical/comedy duo well into their sixties, and thirty years past their prime, thought they needed a bodyguard, but I wasn't going to turn down the job. Although I'd expected it to be easier money than it was.

"Cocksucker!" I heard from behind me, and more muffled profanity.

The manager's eyes were wide at the sounds coming

Splits and Transitions

from inside the room. "Aren't you going to stop that?" he asked me.

"They're paying me to keep them safe from everyone else, not from each other. Brothers tend to fight."

"At their age?"

"I can't fix the world's problems. I can't even fix my own. I'm just keeping my head down, doing my job."

He gave me a dirty look and wandered off.

I'd put on a tie and a suitcoat for the occasion. Under it I had the SIG, two spare magazines, and an ASP expandable steel baton. I doubted they had any fans under the age of fifty, much less dangerous stalkers, but you never know.

Two minutes before they were due to hit the stage the door behind me opened and I stepped to the side. The two brothers—slender, graying hair, both in their mid-sixties—came out, one with a guitar in his hands, one carrying a big bass.

The club had security, bouncers, so during the performance I was able to relax a bit and watch from the wings. The brothers were truly funny, laughing and joking with each other in well-practiced, perfectly-timed shtick, playing a bit of music and singing in addition to telling stories and jokes. Total professionals. You would have never known they'd spent the previous two hours yelling and screaming at each other and throwing things like toddlers having tantrums.

Their set was almost forty-five minutes, and after they left the stage to a lot of applause they walked past me, their smiles dropping like curtains as soon as they were out of view of the audience.

"Could your timing have been worse?" the slightly taller of the two snapped as they headed down the hallway.

"Says the guy who stumbled over half his fucking lines," his brother shot back. They slammed the dressing room door behind them. I went and resumed my post in front of it. They were going back on stage for their second set in just under two hours. From the sounds coming through the door, it seemed as if they were going to spend that entire time fighting.

Forty-five minutes after their second set ended I led them to the limo, parked and idling beside the building. I rode in it with them to their hotel, then went up to the floor with them.

"Thanks," one said to me as they headed into their hotel room, the only acknowledgement I got all night from either of them, and then the hotel room door slammed. And the shouts and profanity resumed.

"Christ," I muttered, and headed downstairs for my car, which was parked in the lot. I was done for the night. Done with the gig, they were flying out of town the next morning.

I'd never worked in Hollywood or Los Angeles, but I knew a few people who had spent a lot of time in the "entertainment industry". So I should have known what to expect, but still.

"Just assume every actor and actress you've ever heard of is batshit crazy, gay, or an asshole. And eighty percent of the time they'll be two out of three," a woman who'd worked as a costumer in L.A. for a few years told me once when I'd asked about her experiences. While this last bodyguarding detail was one of only a few exposures I'd had to the Hollywood crowd, that woman's advice had proven eerily accurate.

As I drove home, the evening's experience made me think of Mike Sullivan and Kerrie Edwards. While her life choices to me were completely alien, she at least appeared to be rational, and trying to live her version of a 'normal life'. Sullivan, on the other hand, was apparently both gay and crazy.

I wondered if he'd ever considered acting. Or musical comedy.

Chapter Twenty

Mike was almost sixty years old, and fat, with a bad knee from tumbling down a flight of stairs while trying to arrest a drunk sometime during the eighties. His days of putting hands on people were behind him, and he'd told me as much. Jerry, on the other hand, was young and in great shape, had seen combat and didn't get rattled, but he was twenty-two years old and looked it. People looked at him and saw a kid. So, even though I knew he could handle an executive protection detail, the next morning I found myself working another bodyguard job.

I was sitting in the lobby of a brokerage firm in Southfield located on the top (fourth) floor of a sprawling office building. Back in the suitcoat and tie, although I'd changed my shirt. They'd fired an employee two days earlier, and apparently it hadn't gone well. He'd threatened to come back and shoot up the place. Kill several people, including the man who'd fired him. They'd filed a police report, but knew paper didn't stop bullets if he was truly serious. So I was parked in the lobby, facing the door, with his picture in my pocket.

Ninety-nine point nine-nine-whatever percent of threats like this were just somebody blowing off steam, venting anger and frustration at having lost a job. Even if they really, truly wanted to murder someone...very few people ever acted on those impulses. So I was there mostly for peace of mind for the employees.

Mostly.

It's the point zero whatever percent of people that fuck it up for the rest of us.

Five o'clock came and went. The employees filed out the front door, some of them scared to look at me, others giving me a friendly nod. I walked the boss man out to his car just before six. He had a small Mercedes sedan, which was a good choice; it showed he was successful, but wasn't ostentatious.

"Are you available tomorrow?" he asked me as I scanned the lot. Many of the parking spots were already empty. A few people were visible here and there walking to their cars. Nobody was paying attention to us.

"If you want me."

He frowned, then looked at his watch. "It's Wednesday. I really don't think Pete's going to do anything...but if he does, it's going to be when he's still pissed. This week. How 'bout you come back tomorrow and Friday. If he doesn't show up by Friday, I figure we're good."

"Sounds like a plan. I'll be here tomorrow when you open."

We shook hands and I watched him drive off, then walked to my car. My heart was hammering in my chest, because after I headed home and cleaned up a bit, I was off to do the scariest thing I'd done in six months, since I was involved in a running gun battle that ended with dozens of dead bodies at a secret CIA compound in Maryland.

I was going on a date.

"Have you been here before?" Heather asked me.

I glanced around the restaurant. Charley's Crab, less than half a mile from my office. Very upscale. "Yes. But I'm not a big seafood guy. I figure for the cost of crab legs or lobster, I can get steak, and I prefer steak."

"But variety is the spice of life." She cocked her head at me, her eyes twinkling. In her red dress she was gorgeous, and got a few looks as we walked in.

"So I've been told a few times."

She smiled. "Are you one of those guys that can eat PBJ sandwiches for lunch and pizza for dinner every day straight for three years?"

"Isn't that every guy?" I asked honestly. That got a laugh.

When the waiter arrived she ordered king crab legs. I ordered a sirloin, which made her laugh again. "You're not drinking?" she asked. She'd ordered a glass of wine.

I shrugged apologetically. "I try not to drink when I'm carrying a gun."

My response surprised her. "Think I might get out of line?" she asked, leaning forward. It took all of my willpower to keep my eyes on her face and not her substantial cleavage.

I smiled. "No, but…think of it as a fire extinguisher, or a seatbelt. You put on your seatbelt when you get in the car, you don't wait until the truck swerves over the center line into your lane."

Splits and Transitions

"You been in a lot of accidents?" she asked, tilting her head.

"More than my share."

"You a bad driver?"

I shook my head. "No, but the roads are full of dangerous people. Some roads more than others."

The waiter returned with her glass of wine. She smiled up at him and thanked him. When he left she took a sip from her glass and put it down. "I suppose they are."

Small talk filled the air while we waited for the food. She was still paying off her school loans. "A DVM costs nearly as much in schooling as an MD to get and you earn less than half as much," she told me. "And you spend half your time putting down animals." I learned she was ten years my junior, which didn't surprise me after seeing her in that skintight dress. She lived in Harper Woods. It was a small bedroom community northeast of Detroit which had an inexplicably high opinion of itself, not unlike "Fashionable Ferndale" a little further west.

After the food arrived she brought up the subject of the dog I'd saved. It had been well over a week, and I'd done nearly nothing to find her a home.

"Do you have a dog?" she asked.

"I did, I don't right now."

"Do you have a fenced yard?"

Her directness was refreshing. "Currently in an apartment. Waiting for the divorce to be finalized. Once it is, then we'll be selling the house, splitting the cash. Then I'll probably buy another house. I'm a house guy, not an apartment guy."

"What's the policy on dogs at your apartment?"

I thought for a bit. "I'm not sure. I know it has to be in

the lease. Wait, I know at least someone there has a small yappy dog. So dogs are allowed."

"Hmm. Well, there might be a weight limit. Small dogs only."

"Really? Is that a thing? I haven't lived in an apartment in forever."

"Maybe you should look into it," she suggested.

I had a wonderful evening, and I think she enjoyed herself as well. She swayed a bit when she stood up, and blinked in surprise. "I guess I shouldn't have had that second glass of wine. They were big."

"And you're tiny."

She smiled up at me as we walked toward the front of the restaurant. She barely came up to my shoulder, even in heels. It was hard not to stare down into her cleavage. We paused by the door. "Do you want me to have them call you a cab?" I asked. I glanced back at the maître d'.

"I don't think that'll be necessary," she said, smiling up at me. "By the time we get done having sex I'm sure I'll be quite sober. I'm not letting this Brazilian go to waste."

I blinked a couple of times. "Well," was all I could think to say. Which made her giggle.

My alarm went off at six a.m. I shut it off. When I rolled back over Heather was awake and looking at me.

"Good morning," I said quietly.

She smiled. "Good morning. What time is it?"

"Six."

She groaned. "I've got to get going or I'm going to be late for work. I've got to head home first for clothes and that's in the wrong direction. Shit, my car's still at the restaurant."

"You don't have spare scrubs in your car?"

"I'm not wearing them over nothing," she said, her eyes laughing. Nothing is exactly what she'd had on underneath the dress. She was as fearless in bed as she was everywhere else. She got out of bed, naked. "Is that what you're into, scrubs? Naked under scrubs?" She sniffed herself. "And smelling like sex."

I sat up a little. "I'm not not into it."

She snorted. "Can you give me a ride to my car?" She headed into the bathroom, but left the door open.

"Sure." As I climbed out of bed I heard her peeing loudly into the toilet and had to shake my head. She was quite something. Practically a force of nature. The only thing that I hated about the situation was that she wasn't the woman for whom I'd put the ring on my finger. But that woman wasn't coming back. I'd apparently made sure of that.

"What are you doing today?" she asked, coming back into the bedroom, talking to be heard over the sound of the flushing toilet. It was hard not to watch her walking around nude. She was very good at it.

"Making sure a guy doesn't shoot up an office full of his former co-workers," I told her as she picked her dress up off the floor. Not that I was still watching her.

"What?"

I shrugged as I pulled on my pants. "Happens all the time. Not guys shooting up the place, but threatening to. When they get fired. Very rarely that something ever happens. If he does ever show up, it'll probably be to beg for his job back. Or yell at his boss. Not go postal. But…"

She glanced over at me. I'd put the SIG on the nightstand, but the holster was still on my belt, on the pants I'd hastily dumped on the floor the night before. I tucked my shirt in, buckled my belt, and then stuck the pistol in its holster. "That's why you're wearing your seatbelt," she said. "Just in case somebody crosses the center line."

"Exactly."

Chapter Twenty-One

Thursday came and went, and Pete Sarkesian never showed up to shoot his boss or any of his coworkers. I cleared that in time to follow Kerrie Edwards from her workplace to school, got in a good workout, and then headed back and took her from school home. No sign of Sullivan.

As much as I still wanted to find Sullivan, there just wasn't enough time for me to work her in the morning and get to my EP gig by the time they opened the doors Friday morning. I spent another entire day sitting in their lobby, listening to horrible soft rock over the hidden loudspeakers.

The career employees, including the boss, stayed late on Friday, so I didn't get out of there until nearly six-thirty. After a healthy dinner of fast food burgers I headed home, did paperwork for an hour to let the food settle, then drove to the gym for an hour of weightlifting, after which I jogged four miles on the treadmill.

Kerrie's house was kinda sorta on my way home, so I swung by there. After ten p.m. the street was dark and quiet. No cars parked anywhere on Muer or on the two streets paralleling it. I headed down Alpine to Big Beaver and was about to make the turn when I spotted a familiar silhouette out of the corner of my eye. An older Mustang, parked in the McDonald's lot.

I threw the Tahoe into reverse with a chirp of rubber and pulled into the lot. Very slowly I crept past the Mustang. Late eighties, check. Tint on the windows, check. Unfamiliar plate, but that wasn't surprising. The car seemed to be empty. I parked where I could see it and also scan the interior of the restaurant. I'd stared at Sullivan's photo enough that I felt confident I would recognize him if I saw him, and I didn't see him. There were a few people in line at the counter, and a few people sitting down, visible from the shoulders up.

Intending to run the license plate, just to see who it was registered to, I reached for my laptop only to realize it was sitting on the desk back at my apartment. I swore, thought for a second, then pulled out my phone. I called another local PI I knew.

"Hey JP, what's up?"

"Jeff, sorry to call you so late on a Friday. I'm out without my laptop and something came up. By any chance are you anywhere where you can run a plate for me?"

"Nope."

"Shit."

"I mean," he told me, "I'm sitting at the home office, trying to edit a report, but the SOS website is down. Has been for a couple hours. But…give me the plate. Maybe it's back up."

I did and waited. The faint clicking sound of a keyboard drifted over the phone. "Nope, still down," he told me. "Sorry."

Splits and Transitions

"Shit," I said again. "Thanks anyway." I disconnected the call and made another.

"Now why would you assume that on a Friday night I wouldn't be too busy to answer your call?" Scott Copley said into my ear.

"Because I've known you for over twenty years. I'm actually surprised you're not asleep already. I need a favor. I need you to run a plate."

"Christ." He sighed. "You know we're not supposed to run plates unless it's for an ongoing criminal case or if we observed the vehicle violating traffic laws."

"The last plate that was on this vehicle was stolen," I said, staring at the Mustang. "At least, I think it's the same vehicle. I'm guessing this plate is stolen as well. He already ran from the cops once. Bloomfield Hills, not your guys. Stalker, if it's him."

"That case you told me about? Give it to me." I read the plate off to him. "Okay, lemmee…I'll call in to dispatch on the phone. Don't want to put this over the radio. Then I'll call you back."

My cell rang a few minutes later. "Plate belongs on a 1994 Ford," he told me. "Registered in Troy. Not reported stolen, at least not yet. Is that what it's on?"

"He's getting smarter, he took one off an older Ford, in the same city, but it's on a late eighties Mustang." I'd done enough research to know the Mustang it was on was very definitely not a 1994.

"Is he violating the PPO?"

"She never could get one. He's been a ghost. I actually haven't seen him here, and it's been," I checked my watch. "Fifteen minutes. Car's empty. At a McDonald's, about half a mile from her house. He's still inside."

"You want some backup? You call the local PD? You got eyes on?"

"No, I haven't seen him yet. I...shit, let me call you back," I told him. I realized I was assuming too much. I tossed the phone down and quickly got out of the Tahoe. I jogged across the lot and entered the McDonald's. There was one person ordering at the counter, and maybe half a dozen seated at tables. None of them were Sullivan. With a frown, I stood there for a few seconds, then headed into the bathroom. Empty.

My frown growing deeper, I stepped out, then pushed open the door to the women's bathroom. "Maintenance," I called out. No response. It was empty as well.

"Hi, can I take your order?" the cheerful pudgy girl behind the counter asked me as I headed back to the front.

"Still trying to decide," I told her. My eyes weren't skimming the illuminated menu, they were checking the faces of the employees behind the counter and moving around the kitchen. No Sullivan. I began to get a very bad feeling.

Heart racing, I sprinted back out to the Tahoe and roared up Alpine. No cars, and no movement by Kerrie's house, and I slowed down as I went past. Lights on in a few of the windows, but I didn't see anyone.

I parked on the street two doors down, grabbed my SIG out of my workout bag, and jogged back to the house. I went up the grass apron between it and its neighbors, on the back side of the attached garage.

My New Balance running shoes grew heavy, then I could feel the wetness soaking into my toes from early dew on the grass. As I rounded the back of the attached garage I thought I heard a muffled shout, but couldn't say from which direction.

There were a few lights showing from the back of the

house, and I approached within a dozen feet—close enough to easily see inside, but not so close the lights inside would illuminate me. The kitchen was empty. I didn't see anyone or anything as I circled around the house to the far side and began to work my way toward the front.

The lights were on in the front room, but the curtains had been closed. I stood near the front corner of the house and looked from the house to the front yard to the street and back. No sign of Sullivan. I pulled out my cell phone and called Kerrie Edwards' cell. I thought I heard, very faintly, a phone ringing inside the house, but she didn't answer. Which was completely out of character for her, especially at that time of night.

My bad feeling grew worse.

I jogged around the back of the house, past the lit kitchen window to a dark rectangle. An open window. I couldn't be sure, but I thought the window led into the main floor bathroom. It took a few seconds with my eye pressed against the screen, but I was able to make out a toilet inside, so I'd remembered correctly. And the window, best of all, was open about four inches. I pressed my hand against the screen, which was barely visible in the night air—simple nylon mesh.

If I'd been wearing my usual pants I would have had a pocket knife on me, and I knew there was at least one knife in the Tahoe, but I didn't want to go back for it. Time seemed to be pressing in on me.

Necessity is the mother of desperation, or whatever, right? I flipped the SIG around in my hand and ran the steel front sight down the screen. It made a tiny "brrriiippp" sound, but when I tested the screen with my fingers it hadn't cut through. I did it twice more, quickly, and then the screen parted for my fingers.

With a gentle shove I opened the window the rest of the way and opened the slit I'd made. It wasn't until I was actually in the bathroom, worrying about falling off the toilet seat as I climbed down, that I actually heard the music. Something soft and slow.

Crap. Was I totally misreading the situation?

Gun up, I approached the open doorway. The hallway went right to the bedrooms, and left toward the kitchen and living room. The bedrooms were dark.

I crept down the dark hallway toward the front of the house, SIG in front of me. The first person I saw was Kerrie's mother, sitting in a chair at the far side of the living room. She was staring at something out of my view, with an odd expression on her face. Another cautious step forward, and I recognized the song—Wonderful Tonight, by Eric Clapton.

One more step and I was moving into the light from the living room lamps. And there was Kerrie, in the middle of the room, slow-dancing with a guy. They had their arms around each other. Her head blocked my view of his face, I couldn't tell who it was.

What the hell?

They rocked back, and forth, turning gently, and then Kerrie was facing me, and I saw the terrified look on her face, the tears running down her cheeks. She saw me and stiffened so suddenly he must have thought she was trying to pull away. He grabbed her tighter with a curt "Hey!" just as her eyes darted from me down to the coffee table at her knee. My eyes followed hers, and I finally noticed the Beretta lying there.

My eyes went back up to see that he had jerked her around so that her back was to me, but I could see his face. I strode out of the dark hallway and his eyes went wide with surprise as he saw me. He let go of Kerrie and bent down for the pistol as I switched the SIG to my left hand. His fingers were just closing over the grip of the Beretta when I punched him as hard as I could in the side of the head.

He went down, his face smashing into the table, and then he was on his back on the floor, unconscious, a big gash across his forehead. I saw a sliver of his skull briefly, and then the split filled with blood, which began running down the side of his head.

I vaguely heard Kerrie in the background, screaming, as I stood over Sullivan. My knuckles where they'd hit him throbbed. Then the screaming stopped.

"Did you kill him?"

"Dead guys don't bleed like that," I said dully, still staring at Sullivan, rage making my temples throb. I shook it off. "You okay?"

I looked at her and she burst into fresh tears, but she nodded. Then she ran to her mother, and they hugged each other and cried together.

Chapter Twenty-Two

"Why 'home invasion'?" Kerrie asked me. She had her arms wrapped around herself and had put on a sweater against the chill. I checked my watch. Well after midnight. I nodded at the last two uniformed Troy officers as they got into their cruiser and backed out of the driveway. The detectives had already come and gone. For a change, I'd never been put in handcuffs as the cops sorted out the scene. None of the rubbernecking neighbors were still outside, drawn by the initial lights and sirens. Past everyone's bedtime.

"He didn't make any specific threats against you, and nobody is quite sure how much weight that California restraining order has here. Even if it has full effect, what's a violation of it, a minor felony? Maybe a year in jail, at most? But first-degree home invasion is a twenty-year felony in Michigan. And it doesn't require any threats or violence, just that he was armed when he broke into an occupied dwelling."

She looked up at me. Her eyes glistened, but the tears

had ended some time before. Her mother, on the other hand, was out cold inside the house, having been given a big Valium by one of the paramedics who'd treated Sullivan.

"Twenty years?"

I shrugged. "I doubt he'll even do half that, but that's eight or ten years you won't have to worry about him. Probably more, once they figure out if that gun's stolen, they'll add that onto the total. And the stolen license plate. And whatever else they can charge him with. He picked the wrong city to do this. Troy cops don't have much real violent crime to deal with, not like Detroit, so they are going to piledrive him." I looked at her. "With his stalking history, they won't even offer him bail, so you won't have to worry about him. He's not getting out. Not for a long time."

He'd barely been semi-conscious when the paramedics finally drove off with him in the back of their ambulance, handcuffed to the railing of the stretcher. That helped with our narrative as there was no opposing point of view for the police to hear. They would get his point of view when they interviewed him from his hospital bed, I'm sure, but whatever story he cooked up would be just that, a story, and they'd see right through it.

She shivered. "Thank you. I mean, if you hadn't come…"

"I would tell you to not worry about it, but I know you will. You'll probably have nightmares. It was scary. He broke into your house with a gun. He's been threatening you for a long time. But now, now he is no longer a threat. Focus on that."

She looked up at me. "You were so angry. Your face… you hit him so hard, I thought you'd killed him."

"All's well that ends well," I said, forcing a smile. I held out my hand. She ignored it, and hugged me. I hugged her back, noticing the slight swelling on the knuckles of my right hand.

"Will I see you Monday, at the police department?" she asked when she backed away.

"Probably." We'd been asked by the Troy detectives to come to the station to give more detailed statements. "Your mom going to be up for it?"

Kerrie laughed. "I'll make sure she is."

"Well then." I gave her a smile and a small wave and headed to my Tahoe, still parked down the street. The SIG was stuffed down the back of my exercise shorts, threatening to pull them down, and I tossed it onto the passenger seat when I climbed in.

Behind the wheel, with the interior light on, I opened and closed my hand a few times, eyeballing my knuckles. I'd hit him as hard as I could, and I'd never been stronger. Not that he hadn't deserved it. I could have legally shot him when he went for the Beretta. But I'm glad I hadn't killed him, for a number of reasons, not least that it would have been in front of Kerrie and her mother. They didn't need to see that. As it was, Sullivan had a probable concussion, and it would take upwards of twenty stitches to close that head wound. At some point he'd probably sue me for the "assault" as I wasn't a police officer and my profession didn't provide me any qualified immunity.

I glanced at my watch. Twelve-thirty. "Christ," I muttered. I started the Tahoe and pulled away. Jerry and I were working a weekend case, a domestic, following a suspected cheating husband as he headed out of town for a 'golfing weekend', and I had to meet him on site at five a.m. The only question was whether I'd be able to get any sleep at all.

Just before eleven a.m. I placed a call to the client. Her husband's maroon Ford Windstar minivan was parked in the driveway of a low gray ranch half a block from me. I had a clear view of it across a small neighborhood playground. The camera I had on the pedestal mount was busy filming the entire front of the house as I made the call, just in case. I popped my neck and rubbed my tired eyes before she answered with a tremulous, "Hello?"

"Mrs. Luccio? It's John Phault."

"Yes? What's happening?"

"We followed your husband to a house on the far side of Chicago. In or right on the edge of Naperville. Single story gray house with an attached two car garage. 1687 Estate Drive."

"That's his friend Gary's house."

"When he pulled up a middle-aged couple came out and said hello. He took a bag inside, and then put his golf clubs in the back of a large pickup in the driveway. It looks like the three of them might be heading out to golf pretty soon, based on how they're dressed."

"Really? I thought for sure…."

"This is where he told you he was going, right?"

"Yes, but I didn't believe him. He's always lying to me. And he was being so shifty…."

"Do you want us to stay on him? Maybe he's got some plans after golfing."

"You said he took a bag in? No, that means he's staying there. I just don't…it's not what I expected. I really thought…" She sighed. "So can I get a refund?"

"Excuse me?" She'd caught me by surprise.

"Since he wasn't cheating."

"Ummm…"

"I gave you a thousand-dollar deposit."

"Yes ma'am, you did. And we, me and another investigator, followed your husband from Roseville to Naperville. That was a five-hour drive, and over three hundred miles. Ten man hours, six hundred-plus miles…I'm not even sure how much of your deposit is even left at this point, I'd have to do the math." And we still have to drive home, I could have added.

"That's outrageous. He's just golfing!"

"Heading back," I heard Jerry say over the walkie-talkie.

I covered the mouthpiece of my phone and grabbed the radio. "Looks like we're done here," I told Jerry. Then I raised the phone once again.

"Mrs. Luccio, you hired me to follow him and find out what he was doing. And I've done just that. An outstanding job of it, if I do say so myself, we followed him across three states, through Detroit and Chicago, and never lost him." And me running on just one hour of poor-quality sleep. "I think you should look at the big picture here. Your husband isn't cheating on you. Instead, he's doing exactly what he said, he's playing golf." I tried a different angle. "How much is peace of mind worth, really?" I smiled, hoping she could sense it through the phone. No such luck.

"It's a thousand dollars! I can't hide that. He's going to find out, and want to know where I spent it. I can't tell him I had him followed."

"I don't know what to tell you ma'am. If we're done here, we'll head back to Michigan, and Monday I'll add everything up and see if you're owed any money or if, in fact, as I suspect, we actually went over budget." I let that hang in her ear.

"I'm not paying you one more dime! I'm going to sue you! I'll take you to small claims court!"

I rubbed my eyes, trying to fight off a headache. "Yes

Splits and Transitions

ma'am, you certainly could do that. But that would cost you even more money, and time, and you'd lose." And then, finally, I was listening to a dead line. She'd hung up.

Thirty seconds later Jerry pulled up next to me, so we were door-to-door in our vehicles.

"Man," he said, "I thought I had an eighteen-gallon gas tank, but I just put nineteen gallons in it. I must have been on fumes."

"I told you to top it off."

"I had over three-quarters of a tank," he said defensively. "So, we're done?" he asked brightly. "I'm getting paid to drive back, right? Time and mileage? Talk about an easy payday." Then he saw my sour look. "What? What'd I miss?"

Chapter Twenty-Three

I was on my way back and halfway through the short, forty-mile stretch of I-94 in Indiana that ran between Chicago and Michigan when my phone rang. I didn't recognize the number, so I identified myself when I answered just in case it was a client, or potential client.

"Mr. Phault," I heard in my ear, the voice warm, almost laughing. "We've never met. But, apparently, you're under a distinctly different impression. My name is Esther Parnell."

I almost veered into another lane in surprise. "Ms. Parnell. Uh…"

"Do you know who I am?"

Frowning, I clamped down on the surprise and put my brain into gear. "Just from what I've heard in the news."

"Hmm. Well, who I not am is Gloria Mitton. And I've never claimed to be her. Not to hire you, not for any reason. And I'm not sure how such a mistake could have been made." It was nice how she didn't exactly accuse me of anything, and definitely nothing so gauche as lying.

I looked all around the somewhat disheveled interior of

my Tahoe, then leaned over and opened the glove compartment. I felt the vehicle veer a bit, and got a horn for my trouble. I sat up quickly and corrected the steering wheel. Faking a cough to give me a few seconds, I then said, "Pardon me if there's background noise, I'm driving at the moment. Ms. Parnell, I'm not sure why you're calling me."

"Don't be coy, Mr. Phault. I have it on very good authority you've told the police that I came to your office claiming to be Gloria Mitton and hired you. To do what, I'm not sure."

"This seems like a conversation you should be having with the police."

"My lawyer is, rest assured. But I was hoping I could have a conversation with you directly. Slander, defamation of character, those are such ugly terms for such an accusation that, unless I'm mistaken, you have no proof. I'm hoping if the two of us talk in person I can eliminate any confusion you might be having. Perhaps we could come to an understanding."

A bribe? It certainly sounded like she was offering to pay me off. Pragmatic. Her thugs hadn't been successful in intimidating me, so now she was trying another angle. It was an amateur move, but then again she was an amateur.

"Mr. Phault? Did I lose you?"

"No, I'm still here. Just thinking. So you'd like to meet?" She was in line for millions in inheritance. Tens of millions. I knew it, and she knew I knew it. I supposed, for a lot of people, money like that, or a piece of it, would be very tempting.

"I think that would be best, don't you? Clear the air. Somewhere private, away from the horrid media types."

"Did you have a day in mind?"

"What is today, Saturday? Sometime later next week I think."

"Monday I have an appointment. Beyond that I'm a bit flexible."

"Excellent. I shall call you back on Tuesday, and we can arrange a time and place for our conversation."

"I look forward to it."

"As do I."

She hung up and I found myself staring at my phone. I set it down, and shut off the digital recorder I'd grabbed out of the glovebox and held in my hand between phone and ear. The recording was not, technically, legal, but I'd done it for my peace of mind more than anything else. I didn't press her for details, because she seemed far too careful to be indiscreet over the phone. It sure seemed like she was hoping to bribe me to change my tune with the cops. Not out of the realm of possible actions for someone in her position even if she was innocent, as I was throwing a blockade up between her and incoming millions.

Except…in all of the video clips I'd watched on the news, it had always been her lawyer talking, not her. This was the first time I'd heard the woman I knew was Esther Parnell speak since Bernard Mitton had died. And while at first the road noise had provided a bit of interference, after a few sentences I could definitively, and without a doubt, identify her voice as belonging to the woman who had sat in the chair across my desk and hired me, claiming to be Gloria Mitton.

I wondered what game she was playing.

Chapter Twenty-Four

Kerrie Edwards and her mother seemed in much better spirits Monday morning at the Troy police station. The detectives had asked me to get there at noon, but I arrived early so I could speak to Kerrie. We were the only people in the lobby. The officer behind the bullet-resistant glass gave us a disinterested glance.

"How are you guys doing?"

At the question her mother still seemed to be fighting back tears but Kerrie gave me a smile. "Good. Good. Not having to worry, knowing he's not out there, stalking me, it's like I can breathe, you know?"

I nodded, then looked at the closed door behind them leading into the station. "Tell them everything, exactly the way it happened. You've got nothing to hide, and did nothing wrong, it's all on him. You've got that copy of the original restraining order?"

"Yeah." Kerrie patted her purse.

I nodded. "Between that, and the reports you filed with

the station before what happened at your house, you're covered, you're golden, no matter what he might say."

"What could he say?" Kerrie's mother said in confusion.

I shrugged. "People lie all the time. He might try to claim you invited him in. He's looking at a long stretch in prison, assume he'll try to lie about everything. What he did, what you did, why he was there…" Then I looked at Kerrie. "I did a lot of work on this for you. You're my client. Is there anything you don't want me to talk about with the police?"

"Like what?"

"Anything at all. Today, they only need to hear what happened Friday night, what got me into your house, why I hit him." I unconsciously lifted my hand and flexed it. "But I did a lot of work on the case before that, there's a lot of background, and you've got client confidentiality. So, anything I need to keep just between us? I can't really think of anything, but you're the boss here."

She shook her head. "I don't think so." She'd caught me flexing my fist. "How's your hand? Are your knuckles still swollen?"

I raised my hand again and we all looked at it. The swelling had mostly disappeared, but my knuckles ached every time I opened and closed my fist. And probably would for a week. "Nearly good as new. Now it's just a reminder to me not to hit people in the head with my hand."

"What are you supposed to hit them with?" Kerrie's mother asked, confused.

"An elbow. A chair. An SUV," I said, with a little smile. She rolled her eyes, and Kerrie snorted.

One of the Troy detectives who'd rolled up on the scene late Friday night opened the door and stuck his head out.

Burns, if I remembered correctly. "Ms. Edwards?" His eyes moved past Kerrie and her mother to me.

"Still want me at noon?" I asked him. He nodded. I looked at Kerrie. "I'm going to go grab a cup of coffee. If I'm not here when you get done, give me a call sometime this week. We'll talk."

She smiled, and nodded. She looked younger. Half the lines on her face seemed to have disappeared, and she walked into the secure area of the station with her back straight, smiling, and holding her mother's hand.

Two minutes after noon Detective Burns opened the secure door to the station and his eyes swept the lobby. "Mr. Phault? We're ready for you. Who's this?" He was looking at my companion.

I smiled. "This is my lawyer." Not Reginald J. Beeman, Esquire. My divorce lawyer only handled divorces, he considered criminal cases something akin to slumming. Beneath him. From what I'd seen of divorces, both as an investigator and participant, he was exactly wrong. A good old-fashioned murder would have been clean and refreshing in comparison. No, I'd brought along Rick Sarlein, who I'd used for years and called whenever I got into trouble with the law. Which was far more often than I liked. He didn't mind, as my cases were "interesting". Plus, he charged by the hour, and "interesting" cases always resulted in a lot of billable hours. Lucky me.

The detective frowned. "Your lawyer? You're not being charged with anything. We're just taking a statement, and clearing up a few points. You don't need a lawyer."

Rick barked out a laugh, and I smiled. "You're funny," I told Burns, and gestured at the open door behind him. "Shall we?"

The dirty look he gave me was priceless.

Speaking to the Troy detectives didn't take too long, especially with my lawyer there to keep my statements short and declarative, and by three p.m. I was down in Detroit, knocking on doors on behalf of Wayne County. Everyone thought of Wayne County as being Detroit, and vice versa, but in fact Detroit took up barely a third of the land area in the county. It was just that Detroit sucked up all the oxygen in the room whenever Wayne County came up. The same was true of the work I was doing. Even though I was working for the county at large, every single door I had to knock on was inside the city limits of Detroit.

Just before six p.m. I made my last stop. I parked just past a small red brick bungalow and looked around before getting out. The thick sheaf of papers stapled together I folded in half and stuck in my back pocket. I was deliberately wearing a Hawaiian shirt, as there are few things less threatening in life than a middle-aged white guy in a Hawaiian shirt. There wasn't much more I could do to make myself look less professional, specifically less like a cop. I'd also thrown on a Detroit Tigers ball cap, in homage to my spirit animal Thomas Magnum. Based on their ages and the neighborhoods they lived in I doubted anyone I was looking for would even get the fashion reference.

The house's lawn had been mowed recently, and there was a pink girl's bicycle on its side by the front porch.

"Yo dude, what up? I think you at the wrong house," said a person I was willing to bet was Anthony Coleman after I banged on his door. He stood there blinking in the bright sunlight, wearing jockey shorts over flip-flops.

"Mr. Coleman, I've got some paperwork for you from Wayne County." I produced the packet and held it out to him.

He backed up half a step, but he didn't let go of the door. "No man, that ain't me."

I smiled. They'd given me a solid description of him—"*black male, DOB 3/14/78, five foot ten, one hundred eighty pounds, tattoo of dagger left forearm, tattoo of Captain Crunch right chest*".

Officially the famous officer's title is "Cap'n", not 'Captain', but I forgave whatever social worker had made the error, because otherwise she'd been very thorough. Even though I wasn't a fan of sugary cereals I recognized the cartoon logo inked onto the chest of the man before me. I pointed the rolled-up papers at the tattoo and gave him a look. He looked down at the tattoo, then back up at me.

"Shit. Fine. What is it?"

"Apparently you're behind on your child support for Jenna. I assume that's her bike out front."

"Man, that bitch, Jenna's mama, she just using the money I give her to buy weed. Jenna's over here most days, I'm the one taking care of her. Feedin' her."

"You should try to get the custody changed then, if that's true."

He gave me a dirty look. "Lawyers for that shit cost money, man. And they won't listen to shit I say until I get right with the support I owe, and I been laid off. Ain't paying shit right now. Friend of the Court ain't no friend, not if you don't got no cash. Even if you do."

"Spending time with her is more important than anything else," I told him. "You're doing that, nothing else matters. So do what you have to to keep your ass in her life. Right now they're just bitching about money. Like a second ex-wife. Make sure it just stays about money."

"Yeah? Shit." He took the papers out of my hand, temporarily subdued. I gestured at them.

"There are phone numbers in there. Make some calls.

Try and get a payment plan set up, or something." I backed off the porch a gave a wave. He frowned and shut the door.

Wayne County only paid me flat rate twelve bucks per each one delivered, and no mileage, but they'd handed me a stack of fifteen. In three hours, plus drive time down to Detroit and back, I'd served eight, now nine with Mr. Coleman. Not bad as hourly wages went, but I knew delivering the remaining six would probably be a grind, requiring multiple trips. I got paid for the effort whether I served the person or not, but the county required a minimum three attempts first.

I got in the Tahoe and drove two blocks, then stopped and wrote the date and time of service, plus a brief description of Coleman. Doing it right in front of their house was a bad idea—once you deliver bad news, get the hell out of there, so they don't have the opportunity to take their anger out on you.

Rush hour traffic was going to be bad, so I took surface streets over and up to Eight Mile. I ran Eight Mile west to Woodward, and took that north into Royal Oak. Pasquale's was a big Italian place just north of Thirteen Mile that had been open since the 1950s. They put fresh chopped garlic on their pizzas, and used the kind of pepperoni slices that curled up in the oven heat and turned into tiny bowls holding pools of delicious grease. I got a large pizza, forgetting their large was the size of everyone else's extra-large, and took most of it home. Then I hit the gym.

Chapter Twenty-Five

My cell phone rang while I was eating lunch. I recognized the number, even though it wasn't programmed into my phone. Or, perhaps, because it wasn't programmed into my phone.

"Phault Investigations and Security, John Phault," I answered, despite knowing who was calling.

"Mr. Phault? Esther Parnell. By any chance are you at your office in…Troy, is it?"

Just from the way she asked the question it seemed clear to me that she knew right where I was. That there was no guesswork in her guess. Which made me suspect that I had eyes on me. Not a good feeling.

"I am, as a matter of fact."

"Would it be convenient if I dropped by, and we could have our little conversation? I find myself in the area."

"I'm eating in today, so come on by."

My office was small. A door led in off the hallway into one room, where my secretary would sit if I had one, and my office was in the back behind that. There was an empty desk in the front room, and a file cabinet, but not much else. It was more space than I needed, but it was the smallest office space the building offered. More and more I was thinking of getting rid of the office entirely as it seemed like an unnecessary expense. Most of the time my office phone was forwarded to my cell phone as I was out working.

Not quite twenty minutes later, long enough to make me doubt my suspicion that she'd been sitting out in the parking lot when she called me, there was a knock at my front door. "It's open," I called out. I was standing in the doorway to my office in back, arms crossed.

Ms. Parnell entered, wearing a very nice floral print summer dress over tan heels and a white hat with a floppy brim as wide as her shoulders. It all looked rather good on her. She took three steps into my office, saw me, smiled, then turned and waited. Ray, he of the heirloom knife, poked his head through the doorway, looking more than a bit nervous.

"She wanted me to come up with her but I told her you said you'd shoot me," he said apologetically.

I almost laughed, seeing him stuck between displeasing his current employer and daring the wrath of someone who'd threatened his life. It was clear he wasn't sure how seriously to take my threat.

"Do I need to shoot you, Ray?" I asked cordially. My smile didn't reach my eyes. And he could probably see the bulge of the SIG on my hip. He looked from me to Ms. Parnell and back.

Finally, with a hint of a smile on her face, she said to him, "Perhaps you could wait in the car."

"That would be best," I assured them.

He gulped, nodded, and was gone.

I returned to the chair behind my desk and sat down. I

Splits and Transitions

shoved the Burger King paper bag off to the side. Esther Parnell took her time strolling in, and first moved to the window. "Not a bad view," she said, touching the glass. As if she'd never been in my office before. This close, in person, whatever few doubts I'd had about who had hired me that day vanished.

"It should be, for what they charge for it."

"Hmm."

She moved over and touched a few awards and framed thank-yous I kept on the shelf along one wall, then, finally, sat down in front of my desk. "Well," she said, smiling.

"Well," I said back.

"It seems we have a situation," she began.

"I don't really see it that way."

She made a sound, then reached over and picked up the coffee mug in which I store pens. She turned it over in her hands as she spoke. "We're in disagreement as to whether I've ever been here before."

"Apparently."

"More so than apparently, Mr. Phault." She set the mug back down with a thump that made the pens rattle. "You're telling the police that I hired you to follow Bernie, claiming to be his wife. Which is absolutely not true. Do you have any evidence of that?"

"Everything I have I turned over to the police. Because if it was his late wife who hired me, her hope of confidentiality is over, my only legal and moral duty is to help solve her murder. And if it wasn't his wife, and the person who hired me lied about who she was, she could have no expectation of privacy," I said pointedly, staring at her. I studied her carefully, just to see if she'd twitch. She just smiled, and pursed her lips. Quite a cool customer, but then she'd always been smooth.

"Do you have any proof that it was me who hired you?" she asked. Twice now asking if I had any evidence of my claim. Interesting. She'd left her mild anger behind and now was going for coolly amused. She picked up my stapler and studied it like it was an ancient artifact from an alien civilization.

"Like I said, everything I had, I turned over to the police. It's their investigation now."

"Which means…no. Hmm." She set the stapler down and looked at me from under the brim of that ridiculous hat. "It seems like it's your word against mine." She tilted her head, and her hat moved like a boat being tossed by waves. "But, still, your accusations are quite upsetting to me. Are you sure there's nothing I can do to help correct your memory? Help you remember things more clearly? It was not me who hired you, and if you could, even at this late date, realize that, and tell the police as much, it would save me so much headache. Your help would be so valuable." She stressed *valuable* just the tiniest bit. And licked her lips.

I leaned back, a thin smile on my face. "Like I said, the police have everything, including a statement from me. And I can't think of anything I'd want to change in that statement." I paused. "For any reason."

She sat there, and I thought I caught the tiniest bit of anger in her eyes, but then she pouted. "Hmm. So…disappointing." She clucked her tongue. "My lawyer wants to sue you for slander. Or is it libel?" Her eyes seemed to twinkle at the thought.

"I doubt that very much. I haven't said anything publicly, so neither libel nor slander applies. All I've done is make a statement to the police during an investigation that is still confidential. No grounds to sue whatsoever. But I'm sure he's told you as much. And told you that if you did sue, then my statement to the police would become public."

She made an abrupt, unpleasant sound in her throat and stood up, her heels clacking on the floor. I stood up as well to be polite. "It appears then we have nothing else to talk about," she said, now seeming distracted.

"I'm sure things will work themselves out."

She put her fingertips on the top of my desk and leaned forward. "I wish I had your faith, Mr. Phault."

I walked her to the door and locked it behind her. When I returned to my desk I opened the top of the Burger King bag, withdrew the digital recorder, and shut it off. Then I sat in my chair and thought.

I wondered just what the hell she'd hoped to accomplish by meeting me, then realized she had accomplished two things. First, she'd looked me in the eye as she offered me a bribe. It hadn't been blatant, but the offer had been there. Talking to someone over the phone is one thing, but watching them, seeing the play of emotions on their face when you say something unexpected, is one very sure way to get a read on them, on how they think and feel about what you're saying. It was very clear to her that I had no interest in taking a bribe.

Secondly, and perhaps more importantly, she'd succeeded in getting her fingerprints all over my office. Mug, stapler, desk.... And Ray could testify to her visit. The date and time was probably marked down in her calendar for any interested parties to see.

She couldn't know whether or not the Detroit detectives had dusted my office for her prints (I doubt the idea even occurred to them, her prints in my office wouldn't prove anything) but even so it showed she was both planning ahead and covering her tracks.

"Son of a bitch," I swore.

Chapter Twenty-Six

I didn't need to be there. Reginald J. Beeman, my divorce lawyer, had made that very clear to me. Several times. And, I knew, the chance of my presence changing anything, altering the inevitability of what was to come, was very small. Infinitesimal. But even infinitesimal is greater than zero. And hope springs eternal, as they say.

Still, I didn't have the opportunity to say anything. In fact, I'd been told several times—by Beeman—to "keep my big mouth shut". Especially in court. So I just stood there as the lawyers and judge went back and forth calmly and professionally.

I hadn't seen Kelly in months. She wouldn't look at me. My wife—very soon to be ex-wife—wouldn't even look in my direction. She didn't look angry. She didn't look sad. She looked…less. Drawn. Diminished. As if there was a shadow on her. I looked at her and tried to see the happy person who'd been there before, whom I'd married. But that person didn't seem to exist anymore.

The anger and sadness fought inside me, and I tried to

think of something, anything, to say or do that could change her mind, get her to stop the proceedings, to listen to me. But…that wasn't anything I hadn't already done. I'd spent hours, hundreds of hours, trying to talk her out of it, and trying to think of ways to get us back to how we had been.

But I knew—there was no way. Not with a dead dog, who'd been like our child, shot in our house by a man she'd been forced to kill. And then her baby, our baby, our son, who'd died when the car she was driving had left the road and flown into some trees. An unfamiliar winding road she'd been driving on in a snowstorm, in whiteout conditions, because she was on the run, in hiding.

And it was all my fault.

Before I knew it she was gone. The background noises had stopped and I looked up. The judge had gone back to his chambers. Kelly was gone, as was her lawyer. Beeman was looking at me with the closest thing to compassion I'd ever seen on his face. In his hands were papers. The signed divorce judgement. It was done.

Over.

I sighed, and shook my head.

"You want to go somewhere, get something to eat?" he asked me.

"No, I'm good." I was anything but, I'd felt better with two broken bones and a concussion. It felt like a part of my body had been removed. A part I very much missed, but that I would never get back.

I was now divorced.

"I've got to get back to the office, get some work done." I nodded at the papers. "That my copy?"

"Yeah." He held it out and I took it, but didn't look at it. There was nothing in there I didn't already know.

"Sorry," he said, and held out a hand. I shook it without enthusiasm. "You did your best." He shrugged.

I looked him in the eye. "I think you're right. That's what bothers me."

After a total seven cups of coffee and no food, by late afternoon my stomach was a cauldron of acid that hated me, but I still wasn't hungry. In fact I felt sick, and what little paperwork and few phone calls I had to make weren't distracting me as much as I'd hoped.

"Hello?"

I hadn't heard the office door open, but I recognized the voice. "Back here."

Kerrie Edwards poked her head through the open door and gave me a smile. "Hey."

"Hey yourself." I gave her my best smile. Apparently it wasn't very good.

"You okay?"

"Just a long day. How about you? And your mother?"

"She's good. We're good. They denied him bail, like you said they would. So he's not getting out."

"Not for a long time," I agreed. I leaned back in my chair and looked at her. "Do your best to move on, and try not to think about him. Every day it'll be easier."

She smiled at me again. "I just wanted to thank you one more time. If it wasn't for you…."

"Don't think about that. Everything worked out. And I'll see you again, if not at the preliminary hearing then at the trial. We'll both have to testify. And your mother. Unless he takes some kind of plea deal. But I don't know if they're even going to offer him one. Home invasion, armed with a stolen pistol?" In Detroit they'd plead him down to a lesser felony in a heartbeat, and he'd be out of prison in a couple of years, especially with no prior convictions. The Troy detectives, on the other hand, had made it clear neither they nor the prosecuting attorney were interested in pleading him down. They had an ironclad case against him, and he had no money for a fancy lawyer to give them a fight.

"How long is that all going to take?"

"The preliminary hearing won't be long at all, but the actual trial, if it goes? You're talking maybe six or nine months before that happens. It'll only take a couple of days when it does go."

"Six or nine months?"

I almost laughed at how outraged she was. "The wheels of justice turn slowly," I proclaimed loftily.

"Crap."

Then I did laugh. "Right you are. But it is what it is. And I'll see you there. Tell your mom hi for me."

As she was leaving I heard voices by the front door, and then Ron Kelly walked in, looking back toward the door. "Yeah, my dad is heading overseas again on Monday," he said distractedly. "You want to come over for dinner either tomorrow night or the next? Maybe we can do some shooting too. And my mom wants to see you, she missed you last time you were over."

"Sure."

"Who was that?" he asked, gesturing. "Client?"

"Yeah."

He gave a low whistle. "Nice legs. She single?"

Between his looks, build, and confidence Ron had bedded more attractive women in high school than most guys did their entire lives, and his years in college had only honed his talents and padded his stats. His recently mangled ear hadn't slowed him down at all. I wondered how many of the young women he was talking up actually believed that it was from being shot in the head, even though that was the truth.

"She's not your type," I told him.

He was still staring back toward the front door. "I don't know about that. Did you see her ass?"

"She's just coming off a bad break-up," I told him. "Stalker."

He smiled. "Easy pickings, then. Rebound sex."

"Not. Your. Type," I told him firmly. "Trust me on this."

Chapter Twenty-Seven

"How often do you practice your draw?" Jerry Phillips asked me after I finished another Bill Drill. It was a simple speed shooting drill—draw and fire six rounds as fast as you can at a silhouette target seven yards away, trying to keep all of your hits inside the center zone. It was a way to evaluate not just the speed of your draw and your trigger finger, but your recoil control and the ability to track your sights between shots.

I could shoot the drill clean—with all center hits—under three seconds, every time, all day long. If I pushed myself I could get my time down closer to two seconds, but then my hits got a little wild. Or maybe a lot wild. I'd watched Jerry run it clean in just over two seconds, and he'd been irritated with how "slow" he'd been.

We were behind George Kelly's barn again. George and his wife were inside the house, preparing a fancy dinner. In two days he'd be flying off to…somewhere. The Middle East, if I had to guess, as his CIA area of expertise was the Arabian peninsula, specifically Syria and Yemen.

I frowned at Jerry. "You mean since I got here today?"

"No, I mean in general. Have you practiced your draw or done any dry-firing since the last time we were out here?"

"A little bit." Usually every time I took my gun out of the holster to put it into my workout bag, or the bedside table, or picked it up off the nightstand to stick in my holster, I practiced my draw once or twice, and told Jerry as much.

"That's not bad, but you should be doing more. Just drawing and dryfiring five, ten minutes a day makes a huge improvement. Practicing your reloads is a good idea too."

"You know, I'm not as good as you, but I don't suck," I told him. I was, in fact, damn good. Better than most everybody. Everybody I knew personally except Jerry, who was exceptional, and Bob Grinnand, who was world-class.

He nodded. "I know, but whoever gets the first hit in a gunfight usually wins. Speed is a tactic."

"So is avoiding trouble."

"You don't seem to be any good at that, either," he said with a smile.

We heard a door slam and looked over to the house. Ron was walking our way with his combat shotgun, a Mossberg 590A1. He'd used it to great effect during our rescue of his father, which also could be accurately described as a cross-country killing spree. Well, not this exact shotgun, the one he was currently holding was a replacement. That other shotgun had been seized by the authorities and had probably been melted, shredded, or dumped into the Potomac. Maybe all three. As had all the guns with which we'd shot people. The technical term for that is "destroying the evidence", but it's not illegal when the government does it for you. At least, that's what I planned to say if I was ever called to testify in front of a federal grand jury, a possibility I still hadn't dismissed.

Ron stopped, and looked toward the front of the property. I followed his gaze, and saw the Oakland County Sheriff's Department cruiser pulling into the driveway.

I looked from the approaching car to the rooftops in the adjacent subdivision and back. Apparently our shooting was ruining somebody's Saturday afternoon.

"Seriously, again?" Jerry said from behind me.

Ron shook his head, took a few steps back to the door, and opened it. "Dad!" he shouted.

Chapter Twenty-Eight

Dinner with Jerry, Steve, Ron, George Kelly and his wife had been a wonderful time. We talked, we laughed, we made some good memories.

On Sunday, however, I wasn't doing so well. I found myself sitting on the couch in my underwear. At noon. I was listless, too unfocused to read or even pick a book to replace the disappointing Hemingway. I couldn't stand the thought of turning on the TV. It would be just so much background noise.

As to the why I was so afflicted with ennui, as the poets might say, it wasn't until I glanced down and saw I was spinning my wedding ring around my finger that it hit me. I looked around the small, quiet apartment. The kitchen, the TV, the dude sitting on the couch in his underwear after noon. This was my life now. No wife, no house, no kids.

I could buy another house, money for that wasn't an issue. As for the wife and kids part of that equation...I found myself adrift from both my past hopes and a future I could easily envision. Would I ever marry again? Was I ever destined to have children? Married with children was how I'd pictured myself at this age, a better looking, slightly less sarcastic version of my father, doling out supportive smiles and stern looks to my kids, as my father had done with me. Instead I was sitting around a shitty apartment, in my underwear, alone.

"Christ," I said, with a big sigh.

I forced myself up off the couch, put on some clothes, threw what I needed into my workout bag, and headed to the gym. It took me close to an hour of heavy weights and self-hate before I threw off the malaise, both physically and mentally. Afterward, instead of my usual slow LSD run—long slow distance, an acronym still stuck in my head from my DEA Academy days—I did a number of quarter-mile wind sprints. Which I absolutely hated, but that probably meant they were good for me.

Back at the apartment I threw my sweat-soaked clothes into the hamper, which was near-full, and took a shower. After the shower I got dressed. I pulled my SIG out of my workout bag and put it into the holster on my hip. I was reaching back into the bag to grab my gold wedding ring, which I always took off when I was lifting weights, when I paused. I'd been about to reflexively put it back on. I lifted the circle of gold out of the small pocket of the bag, sat on my bed, and stared at it.

"Well, shit," I said, and set it on the bedside table. I stared at it for a bit, then forced myself up. I threw all my dirty clothes into the washer and headed out. I wasn't hungry, but I didn't want to stay home alone. I found myself sitting at Starbucks with a large coffee in front of me, perusing the Entertainment section of the Sunday Freep, when my cell phone rang.

Three rings. That's how long I stared at the screen, at

the incoming number, before I answered. "John Phault," I said, but I knew who was calling.

"Mr. Phault, Esther Parnell. Have I caught you at a bad time?"

"Not especially."

"It is Sunday, so I apologize. But I wonder, do you have some free time to meet today?"

I frowned. "About what?" I checked my watch. It was getting late in the day. The Starbucks crowd was thinning out, and I suspected they'd be closing soon. This deep into summer it would stay light for hours, though.

"About our…situation. Something has come to my attention."

"What?"

She made a warm sound. "Something that I really need to show you in person. I apologize for the…what's a good word? Imposition, I suppose, but I really think you'll thank me. This is something…important. To both of us." She let that hang in the air.

"Today?" I glanced at my watch again. Getting on to six p.m. Not that I had anything else to do.

"If you're available. It shouldn't take too much of your time."

I grumbled a bit, but I'm not sure if my phone picked it up. "I'm not at the office."

"No, of course. In fact, I'm wondering if you can come to me? The Ottoman Empire at Gratiot and Metro Parkway. Bernie's original store, the one that started it all. There's something in his office I want you to see. I'm not there right now either, but I could meet you there, say, seven o'clock?"

Once again, I wondered what her angle was, and suspected whatever this was would be a huge waste of my time and probably irritate me to no end, but I admit I was intrigued. "Fine." Maybe she was going to show me a big stack of cash in the safe. Did she know the combination to any of his office safes? That was an interesting question. She obviously had access to at least one of his offices, which I found surprising. I'd followed Mitton there twice the week I watched him.

"Excellent! See you there. Oh, um," she gave a little laugh. "I've been using Ray as security for the past few weeks. The media have been a nightmare. If you see him there, will that be a problem? I don't want there to be any shooting." She chuckled as if the idea of me shooting someone was farfetched.

For someone whom I'd vowed to shoot if I saw him again, Ray sure seemed eager to test the seriousness of my threat. Or maybe it wasn't his doing, maybe it was hers. Seeing how far she could push me. That seemed to fit with her character. As for Ray's testicularly-abused partner, Buddy, he at least had the sense to stay away.

"Fine," I said curtly.

"Wonderful. See you there."

Chapter Twenty-Nine

I spotted the big maroon and blue sign a quarter mile out. *The Ottoman Empire*. Big raised gold letters with a slightly Arabic look to them, just enough to make the name look exotic. Hell, I probably would have been able to spot it, and the store itself, from the moon, it was the biggest thing in the Detroit area short of the Silverdome.

The building was on the east side of Gratiot, just north of Metropolitan Parkway in Clinton Township. I parked right in front of the main doors. I could see lights on inside, but compared to the sunlit parking lot the interior seemed dim. The massive parking lot, which wrapped around three sides of the building, was empty of cars.

As I climbed out of my Tahoe, Ray appeared on the far side of the glass front doors. He unlocked them and held one open. He had an apologetic look on his face once again. "She's in back," he told me, gesturing over his shoulder. The hours were posted on the door, and I saw they'd closed at six.

So…not only did she have access to his office, but she had access to the property after business hours. Interesting.

I walked up the steps and moved inside past him, then waited.

"Hold on, I've got to lock the door," he told me. He had to pull the door tight and turn the latch, and the splint on his hand gave him a bit of trouble. I didn't offer to help.

When he finished, he turned and gestured into the store. "Go on, she's in the office in back."

"I don't know the way. After you."

He pointed. "It's just straight back."

"I'll follow you," I said firmly.

He shrugged and set off. I kept a few steps behind him. The furniture showroom was huge. "Two football fields of savings" was I believe one of Mitton's taglines in his early TV ads, run during local shows like Bowling For Dollars, Sir Graves Ghastly, and Bill Kennedy at the Movies. It wasn't much of an exaggeration, if it was an exaggeration at all.

We wound our way through bedroom and living room sets, dining room tables and recliners, toward the back of the cavernous store. The two of us appeared to be the only people in the place. There were no straight lines in the place. The displays were laid out in such a way as to force you to meander through them and look at every piece of furniture. There were short wall sections set up everywhere as well, to simulate bedrooms and dining rooms. They also cut sightlines and made the huge space feel more intimate.

I saw an open doorway with 'EMPLOYEES ONLY' marked above it ahead, and the sound I'd been hearing grew louder. At first it had been so faint I'd thought it was coming over the speakers, and in fact had difficulty identifying it as music. Drawing close to the office in back, however, it was anything but soothing Muzak.

Splits and Transitions

"What the hell am I hearing?" I asked Ray.

He looked over his shoulder at me. "The Deftones, man. Not a fan?"

It was angry heavy metal, at least to my ears. "No." Jerry probably loved them, had all their albums. I wasn't sure I'd ever heard of them before, but I rarely listened to anything recorded after 1989.

Ray passed under the EMPLOYEES ONLY arch and led me down a hallway to a closed door in back. The thick wood door looked original to the building, and the music, already too loud for my taste, was coming from behind the closed door. When Ray opened the door I got hit with a wall of noise. Beyond him the small office was empty. He walked inside and I followed.

"Where's Parnell?" I shouted at him to be heard over the music.

"You beat her here," he yelled back. "She should be here any minute. I'll go check." He started moving toward the open door.

I gestured at the CD player behind the desk. "Shut off the goddamn—" but then he was through the door and out of sight.

Cursing, I stepped around behind the desk and was reaching angrily to stab the OFF button when something caught the corner of my eye. I looked up to see Buddy rushing through the door, Ray behind him. Both of them had guns in their hands.

"No!" I shouted reflexively, voice lost in the music, sidestepping as I drew the SIG. Buddy fired, the shot going past my arm. I shot him five times in the chest as fast as I could pull the trigger, then once in his surprised face. Behind him, still in the doorway, Ray's eyes went wide. He held a small automatic awkwardly in his left hand.

As Buddy fell slowly backwards, dead on his feet, Ray fired a panicked shot at me and took off running down the hallway. I fired a shot through the doorway at where he'd just been, then emptied my SIG through the wall after him, a string of chest-high holes coring the drywall.

The air was filled with smoke and dust and my ears were ringing from the gunfire. I couldn't hear anything. I blinked, my eyes tearing up, then reloaded and pointed my SIG at the empty doorway. I grabbed the CD player and ripped it away from the wall, and the noise stopped. Making a tactical decision, I took a knee behind the desk. It seemed big and thick enough to stop incoming pistol rounds. Whether it was or not, it was the only cover in the room.

"The fuck, Ray?" I shouted. My eyes dropped to Buddy, just long enough to verify that he was dead, then snapped up to the open doorway. I kept my sights trained on the leading edge of the doorframe, at chest height.

"You know I used to be a cop, right?" I yelled through the open doorway out into the store proper. I didn't know if he was right around the corner or had kept running, but had to assume the worst. "Cops, if they're doing the job right, never want anybody to get hurt. Military, the military on the other hand, has an entirely different perspective. Their job is to kill people and break things. If they're shooting people they're doing their job right. You listening to me Ray? Ray, I've been hanging around with a lot more military guys recently than cops. Like the guy who broke your fingers. The last gunfight I was in lasted…about a week, I guess, and we left a fucking trail of bodies, and I'm still standing. What I'm trying to say," I shouted to the man I knew was out there somewhere, "is that this is not something you want to be doing. It's going to end badly for you. You want to be somewhere else. I've shot enough people. I don't want to have to shoot you. But I will. And I'm good at it." My eyes dropped down, then back up. "Ask Buddy."

Nothing. No shouts, no curses, no insults. If he was making any small sounds I couldn't hear them, my ears were still warbling from the gunfire. And the fucking horrible music.

I had my cell phone in my pocket, but was afraid to take my eyes and attention off the doorway to call 9-1-1. He'd only need half a second of inattention to get the drop on me.

"Shit," I muttered, and moved out from behind the desk. The bullet holes had grabbed my attention. I moved close to that wall and put my eye to one of the holes. It had gone all the way through the wall, and I could see the hallway beyond, but only a tiny circle of it. No Ray. I tried two more holes with the same result.

"Ray!" I shouted, gun up and pointing at the doorway. "Put down the gun. Come out, slowly, where I can see you. See your hands. I promise not to shoot you," I added. It sounded lame even to me. But, oddly enough, I wasn't lying. I'd killed enough people to last me for the rest of my life.

No response.

I couldn't stay there forever. I would need to clear the hallway outside first even if I wanted to hunker down in the office and call 9-1-1.

Biting back another curse, and trying to be as quiet as possible, I moved around behind the desk and approached the door from the opposite side. I was "pieing the corner", as I'd learned all those years ago in the DEA Academy, moving slowly to the side, exposing just a slice of the hallway at a time to my eyes and the muzzle of my gun.

Finally my shoulder was against the wall and I could see half of the hallway over the top of my pistol. No sign of

Ray. Taking a deep breath, I took a quick step through the doorway and cleared the rest of the corridor. Nothing. But there was something on the floor at the far end, underneath the EMPLOYEES ONLY arch. I moved forward, slowly, gun moving back and forth to cover the showroom floor beyond. My hearing was starting to return.

Using the side of the hallway as cover, poor as it was, I scanned the furniture jungle ahead of me, then glanced down at what had caught my attention. Blood, a thick spurt of it. I ran my eyes up the floor, and ten feet out, past a big wardrobe, I spotted a bloodstain in the carpet.

After just a few seconds of indecision, I moved out. Beyond the wardrobe and a hideous modern off-white bedroom set was a wide smear of blood on the floor. Then a bloody handprint on one of the wall sections. Ray's small automatic was lying under the edge of a leather ottoman off to one side. Thirty feet beyond the gun Ray was on his face in a huge puddle of blood, not moving.

I approached him slowly, then knelt down on the blood-soaked carpet. I put the muzzle of my SIG against the back of his head as I checked his pulse. I could feel the warm blood soaking through my pants. My fingertips were beside a ragged hole in the middle of his neck, but blood had ceased to flow from it. He was as dead as he looked.

"Goddammit, Ray," I said with a sigh, fighting back tears.

Chapter Thirty

Cop shows on TV get almost everything wrong, in one way or another. DNA results take at least a month to get back from any lab, and you should assume anything a police procedural show says about physical evidence is wrong. Most criminals are caught because they are either very stupid or doing very stupid things, and blab about it to their friends, family, or the police.

Here's another hot tip—if you shoot someone, much less two someones, even if you're a wonderful human being and did everything right and legal, unless you are a cop yourself you're getting arrested. They'll take your gun (and likely never give it back), and you're going to spend some time in jail while the authorities sort everything out. Because the police are not automatically your friends. They aren't your enemy, either. They're just people doing a job, and that job is to put criminals in jail. After killing two people I was a presumed criminal, until I convinced them otherwise. And, as I was reminded, anything I said can and would be held against me in a court of law.

Sometime late the next afternoon—there was no clock in the room, and when the Clinton Township police had booked me they'd taken all my clothes for evidence, including my watch—I was sitting in my jail scrubs in the uncomfortable metal chair in the interrogation room. Again.

The door opened and Detroit Police Detective John George walked in, a cup of coffee in each hand. He left the door open. "Here," he said, hoisting one of the cups before setting it on the table before me. "For stationhouse coffee it doesn't suck."

I'd asked the Clinton Township detectives the night before to call him, and had spoken to him once that morning, in a very crowded room filled with detectives and at least one lawyer in addition to my own, but had heard nothing since.

"Security camera at the Arby's next door shows you arriving, and that someone let you into the store, but that's it. All the cameras inside the furniture store were conveniently off. So if you hadn't accidentally bumped the pocket holding your digital recorder and turned it on, we'd have no record of what went on in there. Even though the music makes it very difficult to hear what was said right before those first shots were fired." He took a sip of his coffee. "Difficult, but not impossible."

From the way he'd said 'accidentally' he knew it had been anything but. Michigan law made it illegal to record people without the consent of all parties, unless you had a warrant. In this case I figured the value of the recording would outweigh everything else, especially since I kept to my story that I'd accidentally activated the recorder as I'd climbed out of my Tahoe. It was still recording as the responding officers pulled it out of my pocket.

"Had a busy day?" I asked him, and took a drink of the coffee. He was right, the coffee didn't suck, although it probably wasn't the best dietary choice on an empty stomach.

"Served the search warrant on both the dead guys' places. Haven't found much of anything, yet."

"No?" The hangdog expression on my face made him smile.

"No. But the girlfriend of one of them had a lot to say. As did the manager of the furniture store." He took another sip of coffee, and when he lowered the cup, his smile was even wider. "Oh, he had quite a lot to say. Apparently he and Ms. Parnell were quite…intimate. He was angling for a big chunk of that money, and was more than willing to give her access to some of Mitton's properties. Attempted murder, however, was apparently more than he could stomach. Whether or not he knew about it ahead of time is the question, but he's giving us a lot to work with."

My lawyer Rick Sarlein stepped through the doorway with a man I knew was an assistant prosecuting attorney with Macomb County. Rick gave me a smile and a nod.

I looked back at George. "Enough to get Parnell? On conspiracy to commit, or as an accessory?"

"Here's hoping."

"On me, or Mitton?"

"Both. Maybe." He gestured at the door with his cup. "Free to go."

"He will of course make himself available to you whenever you have any questions," my lawyer said to the county attorney.

I stood up and held my hand out to the DPD detective. "Thanks, George."

He took my hand. "Call me Ringo," he told me. He

looked me in the eye and without letting go of my hand said, "Hanging out with military guys? Trail of bodies? The last gunfight you were in lasted a week?"

I knew he had to have researched me at some point during our interactions. I'd killed a number of people over the years, but the most recent incident to which I'd been referring had supposedly been scrubbed from local law enforcement databases. But that didn't mean he couldn't have talked to a few people. "Just saying whatever I could to get him to give up peacefully."

He gave me a dubious look, and finally let go of my hand. "Uh-huh."

My bloodstained clothes had been taken as evidence, and I'd never get them back. The same was likely true of the SIG. When my phone was returned to me I saw I'd missed fourteen calls from Jerry and Mike, and had six voicemails. I called Jerry first, without listening to any of the messages. I'd scheduled myself with him that morning for a surveillance. I walked with my lawyer, who'd offered to drive me back to my vehicle.

"Jesus Christ, you okay?" were the first words out of Jerry's mouth.

"Yeah. Just had an emergency come up. But I'm fine."

"You had me worried there. I was about to break off, the claimant hasn't done shit all day. Probably a good thing you weren't here. You want me to stay longer?"

I checked the time. "No, go ahead and kill it." My automatic phrasing made me pause. Jerry didn't notice.

"I was going to head over to your house, see if you fell in the shower and broke a hip. I hear that's what happens when you get old. No, wait, you're in an apartment now, aren't you?"

We reached Rick's Mercedes, a large chunk of which I'd

personally paid for, one hour at a time, and he unlocked the doors with a beep. I climbed into the leather passenger seat.

"Yeah." I paused. "You want to come over tonight? Maybe we can grab dinner somewhere."

Maybe he heard something in my voice, maybe not, but he answered immediately. "Absolutely. Just give me an address and let me know when to show up."

"And..." I began, something suddenly occurring to me, "where's the best place around here to pick up a new SIG 226?" Rick glanced over at me and frowned. I ignored him.

Jerry didn't say anything for a few seconds. He had the experience to know exactly why I was asking. "Seriously?" he finally said.

I sighed. "Yeah."

"Double Action, in Madison Heights. I know Al, one of the owners. I'll introduce you. We can go there first, then get something to eat. And you can tell me all about it."

Chapter Thirty-One

"Hey," I said.

"Hey yourself," Heather replied, smiling up at me. As I returned her smile the wall of animal noise around me faded. She cocked her head, a twinkle in her eye. "Friday or Saturday night. Either or maybe both, depending. You free?"

I blinked. "Both? Um, uh, no. No plans. You mean like a date?" I held up my left hand. There was no wedding ring to be seen. I'd put it away in a drawer, for good, that morning. That small little physical act had gotten me far more emotional than it should have. "Freshly divorced."

She smiled. "Good. Dinner and a movie. This time I pick. Not that I didn't love the seafood."

"O…okay. Movie?" I had no idea what was even playing. I hadn't been to movie theater in eight or nine months.

"Yeah. I want to go see Finding Nemo. I hear it's great."

I frowned. "The animated one? Talking fishes?"

She laughed. "I'm a vet. Animals come with the territory." She grabbed my arm. "Come on." She pulled me along. As we walked she looked up at me. "How was your week?"

"A bit crazy, but better now." I smiled down at her.

"Yeah?"

"Yeah."

The noise from the animals in the lobby faded, but as we moved into the building the noise from the animals in back rose. Mostly dogs barking. Incessantly. "Is it like this all the time?"

"Like what?"

"The noise."

She laughed. "I don't even hear it anymore. But no. They're getting fed. Gets them all excited."

"I know the feeling. I've started barking at a few restaurants."

There was a young girl in a smock doling out food to the animals. We moved past her and stopped in front of a cage. The puppy inside was busily eating kibble out of a small bowl.

"She looks a lot better."

Heather nodded. "We took the sutures out a while back, and the cone came off a few days ago."

"Hair's growing back. Still looks like she got attacked by a lawn mower."

"She's got beautiful hair." Heather cocked her head. "Mixed breed, but she looks to be more husky than anything else. Which means she won't mind the cold at all, but anything over seventy degrees and she'll be panting. Her coat's got two layers."

"I think she's bigger, too."

"That's what happens when you feed them." I gave her a look and she laughed. "She'll get to be at least forty pounds, but beyond that it's a guess. Most huskies aren't as heavy as they look, though, because the hair is fluffy and adds bulk."

"Like the girls I dated in the eighties." Heather snorted.

Bowl empty, the puppy sniffed all around for errant crumbs and, finding none, finally noticed there were people outside her cage. She pressed her black nose against the wire, snuffling loudly.

Heather opened the door and pulled her out. The puppy squirmed excitedly, and licked Heather's face as soon as she got in range. Her tongue was pale pink. "You can barely even see the scars," I observed.

"As soon as the hair's done growing back in you won't be able to see them at all. Here, you hold her." She handed me the puppy without waiting for a response. She wasn't as heavy as I was expecting. When I looked down at her she licked my nose, which made Heather laugh.

"Pretty calm, as you see," Heather said, gesturing at the dog in my arms. The puppy wasn't squirming to be let down, she was satisfied, at least for the moment, in my arms. She looked around the room, nose sniffing energetically. Her ears twitched whenever one of the other dogs would bark. Then her mouth opened in a huge, tongue-curling yawn. It ended with a quiet "yowp" sound that made her blink in surprise. She looked up at me suspiciously, as if I was responsible.

"That was all you," I told the puppy, shaking my head. She probably didn't get much sleep with all the barking. One noise would set the whole room off.

"So?" Heather said expectantly.

I pulled the leash out of my pocket and held it up.

"Good," Heather said, nodding and smiling. "Good. I need to get her a collar to attach that to, hold on." She headed off.

Splits and Transitions

I looked down at the puppy in my arms. I would have to delegate a lot of the surveillances coming in, at least for the next six months or so, as I knew puppies couldn't be left alone for eight or ten hours at a time. Well, not without making a huge mess. Maybe I could take her to the office with me. Did my office building have a policy on animals? Probably, but I'd ignore it until somebody said something. And I'd need to train her. Kelly had handled all of that with Oscar. New territory for me. In a lot of ways.

At the thought of my previous dog my heart dropped, and the puppy took that moment to lick my chin. I looked down into her ice blue eyes. "Yeah?" I said. She licked me again. Puppy licks work very well as an instant antidepressant.

Heather returned. "She's had all her shots, and we spayed her as well," she told me as she fitted a narrow collar around the puppy's neck. She took the leash from my hand and attached it to the collar, and I set the dog on the floor. She started enthusiastically sniffing everything, her tail wagging.

"Have you thought of a name?"

I hadn't, but one popped into my head unbidden. "Raven," I told Heather.

She nodded. "Nice. Let's head back up front. You've got to fill out a little paperwork, and we need a check or credit card to cover the spaying."

We walked toward the front, the puppy doing random patterns in front of us, sniffing everything. "You should put the cost of the other surgery on my bill too," I told her. "Whatever it cost to fix her head up and take care of her the past few weeks."

Heather stopped and looked at me. "You didn't shoot her."

"No, but it's the least I can do."

Heather's smile grew warm and soft and she squeezed my arm. She led me back out to the front desk. "Linzee," she told the receptionist, "the paperwork for this little girl should be right...there." She pointed to a spot on the cluttered desk, then looked at me. "I've got to get back to work. We'll figure it out and send you a bill for the other stuff." She rose up on her tiptoes and gave me a kiss on my cheek. Linzee gave us the side-eye but didn't say anything. "I'll talk to you later," Heather said, and disappeared into the back.

Linzee set a clipboard on the counter in front of me. "I need your signature, an ID, and a credit card," she told me. As I was digging my wallet out, she added, "So you're the hero?"

I shook my head and handed over my driver's license and a Visa. "No, just trying to do the right thing."

Linzee looked about twenty, with very dark skin. She appeared slightly taller than she was wide, and overflowed the chair she sat on. She gave me a dubious look as she stood up to collect the clipboard and my cards. "Mm-hmm."

Raven was pulling steadily at the leash, trying to reach the other dogs in the waiting room. But she had no weight behind her efforts, and her paws slipped on the tile floor as if it was ice. It was very cute.

"Here you go."

I collected my cards and the paperwork and got everything put away while dealing with a tugging leash. Then I looked down. "You ready to go?" I asked Raven. The puppy stopped her tugging and looked up at me. She cocked her half-shaved head, ears flopping over.

I gave the puppy a shrug. "It's kinda new to me too, kid, but we'll figure it out."

Next in the James Tarr Conspiracy Thrillers series

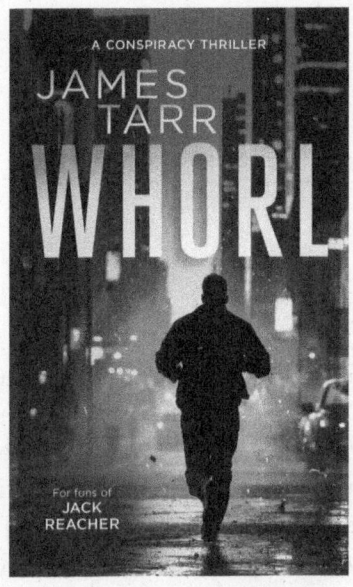

vinci-books.com/whorl

Fingerprints don't lie.

A routine background check sends shockwaves through the FBI when a lab tech discovers Special Agent candidate Dave Anderson's fingerprints match two other people already in the system.

Turn the page for a free preview…

Whorl: Chapter One

PART I: THE ONE-PERCENTERS

David Anderson turned onto Third Street and pulled his beat-up Jeep Cherokee into the gravel parking lot. The lot was small, and enclosed by a rusty eight-foot chain link fence topped with menacingly shiny concertina wire. The electric gate was on rollers, but it was always left open. He doubted whether the motor would even work if they tried it, but they never really had any problems.

Technically the lot was under surveillance, but he'd seen the black and white picture the camera on the roof fed to the TV in the control room. It might as well have been one of those ultrasound pictures of a baby in the womb. They looked like moonscapes; he could never see the baby, and in the camera's fish-eye lens he couldn't even recognize his own car on the TV screen.

He climbed out of his car and stretched. The sun was just coming up over the buildings on Cass, and shadows still covered most of the ground around him. Outside the lot on one side was a building with impressive stonework that had probably been built in the twenties or thirties. It was now a blackened, windowless hulk that would look at home in a zombie movie.

The vacant lot on the other side sported knee-high grass that would be a foot taller in a month. The city used to do a better job of mowing the vacant property, but there was just so much of it, and so little tax money coming in anymore, that pretty much anybody who could get out of the city was gone. Too much space, not enough money, not enough people, and the ones who were left….

Weeds grew along the fenceline, some of them nearly as tall as he was, and there were a few maple saplings growing in the corner. It was ironic; the closer Detroit got to death, the greener it became. In nature things usually worked the opposite way.

There was only one person on foot that he could see, a woman heading west down the sidewalk. Deathly skinny, from her stained, crumpled sweatshirt and jeans it was hard to tell if she had been in a fight or just up all night. She wasn't wearing a bra, he could see that, whether he wanted to or not. Mostly not. She took one look at him and his freshly laundered and pressed uniform shirt, and gun, and didn't bother to proposition him. Dave was still young enough that being that close to a hooker, even one who looked like she had several infectious diseases, gave him a little naughty thrill.

He waited for her to pass, then did a quick check for traffic. With hardly anybody living in the area the cars were few and far between, but in a city where the cops ran from one violent crime to the next, speed limits were almost as big of a joke as stop signs. Street clear he headed across the street to the nondescript tan building. Two stories, concrete, with a single overhead door (closed) and a single pedestrian door. No company name or sign indicating what the business was, although all anybody had to do to find out was look into the fenced-off yard on the west side of the building. Or watch the trucks coming and going all day.

Ten foot chainlink around the yard, no rust on this fence, topped with overlapping coils of razor wire. Whoever came in last, unless they were in one of the new trucks, had to park in the outside yard. In the summer it wasn't bad, but in cold weather he usually had to scrape the ice and snow off himself. Though it was late May the early morning air was a little chilly, but he'd left his uniform jacket at home. It'd be eighty by noon, hotter inside the truck.

With his fingers touching the handle Dave looked up into the camera above the door. After a few seconds of nothing, he hit the doorbell and grabbed the handle again. Whoever was manning the controls finally spotted him and buzzed him in.

Inside, the building resembled a warehouse more than anything, which made sense considering it was nothing more than a glorified garage attached to a big safe. The airy space echoed with the shouts of men and the revving of truck engines. Dave hurried up the gently sloping ramp just in case one of the scarier drivers was on his way out. There'd been a couple of close calls, on the ramp and in the loading area, but somehow nobody had been run over. Yet.

He punched in, then looked around for Aaron. He found him at the window, checking out their load. Everything was locked up overnight in the vault. Outside the vault was the office, with the pass-through window. All the messengers called the small room where they picked up and dropped off their cash the Fault Room, because if their load was ever found to be short, that's where it was discovered, and it was always their fault.

"I take it I'm driving today," Dave said as he watched

Aaron counting the boxes of pennies on his steel cart. In the armored car business the messenger, and the messenger alone, was responsible for the money. He signed for the load in the morning, had to keep track of what he picked up or dropped off, and get signatures for everything, and then turned whatever he had left into the vault at the end of the day. All the driver did was drive.

"Fuckin' Huntington," Aaron said, kicking one of the penny boxes. "I thought I was going to have a light load today, until I saw their twenty boxes of fucking pennies." Aaron, like most veteran messengers—the honest ones at least—had long ago stopped thinking of his cargo as money. To him it was just weight. Pounds, not dollars. Cash was good, he could do cash all day. Paper, paper, paper. It was the coin that killed you, especially around the holidays. Christ. First week of December, every day he had two hundred boxes of coins to deliver.

"Are you done bitching?" Joe asked through the window. "I want to finish checking you out before I die of old age. Huntington cash, one, for four hundred thou even." He hoisted the canvas bundle onto the steel shelf and shoved it toward Aaron, who spun it around so he could check the tag against his paperwork, then yanked it down onto the cart. All twenties inside, by the size of it.

Joe was nearly six-foot-six and slightly older than God, at least if you believed what he said. He practically had to fold himself in two to look out through the vault window. A few wispy white hairs dotted his age-spotted skull, and he reeked of tobacco. His yellow and usually bloodshot eyes were huge behind Roy Orbison-looking glasses. He wore his uniform pants in true geezer chic style, pulled up into his armpits, revealing white, droopy socks and legs as skinny as toothpicks and damn near the same color. His uniform shirt had last been white sometime during the Nixon administration.

"You're going to outlive all of us, you pissy bastard," Aaron said good-naturedly. He turned to Dave. "You'll never guess what we've got today," he said with a smile. It was a real smile, he seemed highly amused by something, but the look on his face would have scared most people away. Dave figured that was why Aaron had never been robbed—he looked slightly insane.

Jet-black hair, a little too long so it touched his collar, and a true '70s pornstar moustache that needed a trim. Bad teeth—not horrible, but two years of braces would have done wonders for him. Of course, his mother had barely been able to pay the rent on the trailer when he was growing up, so braces were out of the question. So were regular visits to the dentist. Slightly buggy eyes, and an intense staring gaze that made Dave think of a serial killer. A real one, not a Hollywood archetype. One glare and even the freakiest-looking loiterer left the area when he was unloading the truck at a stop. Surprisingly Aaron wasn't ugly but rather handsome, in a bad-boy sort of way, and could be very charming. He did his best to bed every teller better-looking than a Rottweiler, and had succeeded more often than he'd failed.

The two of them had never been robbed while working together. Dave figured it had to be because of the way they looked. Aaron glared at any male like he was wondering how their livers tasted, and Dave always paid attention and looked competent. "Short-haired college boy" is how he was usually described, with "suburban white boy" following a close second. Not only was he always wearing a clean, pressed uniform, whenever they were at a stop he actually scanned the area for possible threats. Not like some of the drivers the company had, that's for sure.

"I shudder to think," Dave said.

"A third man."

Technically, every truck, every day, should have a third man, a guard who would exit the truck and stand beside the messenger as he loaded his dolly, follow him wherever he went, but most customers didn't want to pay for the extra service.

"How do we rate?"

"New guy, you're supposed to train him," Joe said through the window.

"Christ. So am I driving?" Dave occasionally worked as a messenger, but because he was only part-time, and his schedule was the same every week, he usually worked with Aaron. Drivers weren't supposed to get out of the vehicle, but Dave always wore body armor under his uniform shirt, just in case. Aaron wore a vest and plate, every day, religiously.

"Yeah, I don't trust this monkey in traffic, but he'll do fine as a bullet-catcher," Aaron said.

"Jesus, Aaron." Dave looked around to see who had heard him. "Where is he?"

"Out at the truck. We've got the Beast again today."

"Well, at least it runs." *Even though it doesn't have air conditioning, or a radio, or shocks*, he added silently.

"Runs, it's fucking *Christine*, that thing's never going to quit."

The vault door banged open, and one of the supervisors barreled out. "Jesus Reg!" Dave exclaimed, jumping out of the way just before the cart wheel would've run over his foot, undoubtedly breaking something. "What's your hurry?"

"Gotta be done by three, got Tigers tickets," Reg called back over his shoulder. His chunky legs pumped behind the cart, heavily laden with coin.

Dave left the fault room and stood looking for the truck. He spotted it near the back of the garage, and was pleased to see it'd been parked indoors overnight. The garage walls were painted grey over an odd shade of blue, except for the big patch at the back where Stuey'd run the coin truck through the cinderblocks. Drive, Reverse, whatever. Half again as long as the other trucks, the coin truck had a beefed-up suspension to handle its heavy load. Stuey and Jeff went back and forth to Ann Arbor every day with several tons of coin. The two of them were as unlikely a pair as Dave could've imagined, but had worked the run together for years without a hitch.

Jeff came rolling by on a forklift, sporting a full pallet of $1000 quarter bags from the coin vault. Instead of counting the coins they just weighed the bags, and the scales were accurate to within one quarter. The forklift beeped loudly no matter which direction it was heading, forward or back, but still about once a year somebody managed to hit it with a truck. Its yellow skin was scraped and dented like it'd been mauled by a dinosaur.

Stuey was standing at the back end of his truck, watching as his partner raised the pallet up to the open door. He was a big black man, a heavy gut straining at the suspenders holding up his back-support belt. His "white" uniform shirt was uniformly grey, and his hair, always a bit too long, was spotted with grey to match. Dave had always thought Stuey looked a little like Don Cornelius of *Soul Train* fame, but the resemblance ended whenever Stuey opened his mouth.

"Ey bi' mannnn, whatcha at?" Stuey called out to Dave

as he walked up. He had to shout to be heard over the forklift. "Lookin' sharp, lookin sharp, gotta sweet mama waitin' fo ya affa work t'day?" He cackled and looked to Jeff for a reaction. Jeff smiled but never looked away from the pallet as he threaded it through the doorway, an inch to spare on either side. Stuey's unique speech pattern had been termed *Alabama Marble-Mouth* by Aaron, a description which hardly did justice to the abuse Stuey heaped upon the English language.

"No, I'm all gussied up for you, you big teddy bear," Dave said with a grin. He quickly scooted around the back of the forklift—Jeff was notorious for abrupt changes in direction—and kept on toward his truck. Stuey cackled even more, and glanced up at Jeff, who was lowering the pallet onto the enclosed bed of the truck. Even with the heavy duty springs the truck bed sunk two inches under the weight of just one pallet.

"Teddy bear," Stuey said with a smile. "Heh heh heh."

Jeff was in his late forties, a chain smoker with sandy brown hair going grey and a handlebar moustache. He would've looked more at home in a string tie and cowboy hat, and still had some of the twang, even though he hadn't been back to Arkansas in twenty years. "Yeah, that's just what you are," he said drily, looking down at Stuey.

"Bi' black sessy teddy bear," Stuey rolled on with a smile. "Good fo *allll* the ladies, givvum some a dat Teddy Bear blacksnake, da ol' one-two, dey be smilin' like it's Christmas." His deep voice sounded like gravel down a metal chute, and his three-pack-a-day habit wasn't making it any clearer. Most people couldn't even understand him, which was just fine with Stuey. He liked to be left alone as much as possible.

Reg Coleman was throwing the heavy coin boxes into

the back of his truck like a madman. It reminded Dave of news footage he'd seen of people frantically tossing sandbags onto the banks of a rapidly rising river. Pete, his regular driver, just stood out of the way, grinning. He gave a little wave to Dave as he passed. They were both part of the same sub-species at Absolute, white boys from the suburbs looking to get into law enforcement. Pete had his name on a couple of hiring lists, and would probably be working for one police department or another by the end of the year.

Dave reached "The Beast" and looked around for the third man. Nowhere to be found. What a surprise. One of the oldest trucks in the company, 1555 was also the biggest, second only to Stuey and Jeff's coin truck. Although the exterior had been recently painted, and the diamond-plate polished, the interior of it was as inviting as a turn-of-the-century jail cell. During winter the heater only worked when the truck was moving, and in summer the steel got so hot Dave couldn't lean his forearm against the door for more than a few seconds. Anything over eighty-five degrees outside and the truck turned into a rolling oven. Technically the air-conditioning worked, chugging out cool wisps of air so faint they were imperceptible six inches from the unit, but there really was no recourse. The tiny gunports wouldn't stay propped open when they drove, and armored car windows don't roll down.

Aaron arrived, pushing the cart. He tried the side door of the rear compartment and found it was open, and the two of them began transferring the cart's load into the back of the truck.

"I think I've been working here too long," Dave told Aaron.

"Why?"

"I just had a conversation with Stuey, and I understood every word he said."

"Jesus Christ. Get out, get out now, while you still can."

Squatting in the open doorway, Dave looked up and saw who had to be their third man approaching. He looked barely sixteen, but by law had to be at least twenty-one since he carried a gun. The fat gave him a baby face, and a build like Santa. He looked nervous and eager to please. Dave tapped Aaron and nodded at their third. Aaron turned around.

"Where the hell have you been?"

A guilty look. "The bathroom."

"Well Christ, don't just unlock the truck and walk away, we're not delivering fucking milk you know."

"I—"

"Forget about it. This is Davey, my partner. He may look like a brainless college kid, but he knows what the fuck he's doing, which is more than I can say for most of the humps around here, so you listen to him."

"Gee, thanks," Dave said. He saw the kid was carrying one of the company guns, a battered Smith & Wesson M&P revolver that had probably been new during the Truman administration, in a cheap padded nylon holster. Probably loaded with the company ammo, too. He shook his head. Kid would be better off with a baseball bat.

"What's your name? Mo? That short for something?" Aaron asked.

The black kid squirmed. "Elmo," he said, looking at the floor.

"No shit? As in '*Tickle Me*'? Hey, don't knock it, at least it's a real fuckin' name, not like Ikea or something."

Dave blinked and shook his head in confusion. "Ikea?" They'd opened up a big store not too long ago in Canton.

"You want to bet money that there isn't a little girl born in Detroit the last few years that ain't been named Ikea?" Aaron challenged him. "I know someone at Wayne County, they can do a name search on the birth certificates. Fifty bucks on it? Hundred? No? How bout we limit it to the past two years?"

Dave shook his head. "I'm not taking that bet."

"Bout the best way to shout 'I'm stupid' to the world, you ask me, give your kid a fucked-up name."

Dave stared at his co-worker. "You're just a regular politician, aren't you?"

"Hey, I'm just a fuckin' observer."

"You'll have to forgive my partner, he was raised by wolves," Dave told the new kid, who wasn't sure what to make of their exchange.

"Taylor-tucky trailer trash, born and bred," Aaron said proudly. "Dave's gonna drive today," he told Mo. "You'll be my guard. They tell you what a guard's supposed to do?"

"But they said—"

"I don't give a fuck what they said. I'm the messenger on this run, which means I'm the boss once we get out that door. I tell you to sit on the hood and wave your cock at the hookers, you do it. Driving an armored car ain't like regular driving, and I'm not going to have you behind the wheel your first day out. Dave'll show you how it's done. Every run's different, but you'll get the idea. He's good. He can make this beast *dance*. Hell, you know he got this thing airborne once? Four feet of fucking daylight under the tires." Aaron loved telling this story. Mo's mouth opened in awe and he stared at the truck towering above them.

"Not on purpose," Dave assured him, shaking his head.

Splits and Transitions

Dave wrestled the big truck up onto the sidewalk in front of the ugly gray building and parked. They had eight feet of clearance between the truck and the building, with the driver's side of the truck flush with the curb. There was parking allowed on the street, but Aaron preferred it this way, and knowing his reasoning Dave wasn't sure he was wrong. Dave looked back through the steel mesh at Aaron, then out the windows. As Mo went to open the passenger door and jump down Dave stopped him.

"I'll get out here," he told Mo. "You just stay in the cab."

"You sure? Why?"

"Because for one thing you were about to open that door, again, without looking around," Aaron chastised him from the back. "For another, this is a hot location."

"Hot? You mean, like robbery attempts?"

"Not so far, but between the cars and the foot traffic you need to keep your head on a swivel here. Vernor and Junction, baby, *estamos en el ghetto Mexicano*."

"What?"

Aaron just sighed. Most of the signs along Vernor were in both English and Spanish, and of the ones that were in only one language, most of those weren't English. It still wasn't as bad as Dearborn, though, he figured. No women dressed as ninjas walking around, all the signs looking like they'd been vandalized by scribbling toddlers.

"You see who's having lunch again?" Dave asked his partner with a jerk of his head.

Aaron glanced back over at the blue Michigan State Police Dodge Charger parked in front of the coney island across the street. Even after all these years they still only had one big red gumball light on the top. "Yeah, I saw 'em. Fucking ramp roosters, they practically live there."

"That's good, right? That the cops are there? So it scares away anybody thinking about robbing us?" Mo looked back and forth between the two of them. Dave let Aaron take it.

"Maybe," Aaron said. "As a general rule, though, cops get the fuck out of the area when they see us, *just in case* there's a robbery attempt. They don't want to get caught in the crossfire. That's why you probably won't see them come out and leave while we're sitting here. Our stop here is, what, ten, fifteen minutes? And we've seen an MSP car there probably two dozen times over the years. How many times have they finished lunch, walked out, and driven off while we've been parked here? Dave?"

"Never."

Aaron looked at the new guy. "Never. That, dude, is what they call a statistical anemone." He looked back at his partner. "You see anything?"

"Just that guy sitting in that piece of shit gray Chevy down there in front of the thrift shop, been there since we rolled up." There was a decent amount of foot traffic on the sidewalk on both sides of the street, but other than the occasional glances no one was paying the armored car much attention, or loitering close by.

"Yeah, I saw him." All the cars in this neighborhood were pieces of shit, although half of them were layered with extra chrome or gold or decals of the Virgin Mary on the back window or some such. Hadn't these people ever heard of stereotypes? Aaron's mouth spun up again. "What the hell is with all the 'In Loving Memory of Pablo' or whoever the fuck family member who died, commemorated by a big sticker on the back window of their car? What's in loving memory, the sticker? The back window? The car? Did they buy their shitty Buick with dead Pablo's life insurance benefits? I swear to God." He shook his head, then peered out the dirty windows to either side, studying the cars and pedestrians. "Okay," he said to Mo, "what's company policy if you're a driver and someone grabs your messenger, tells you to open up or they're going to shoot him?"

"Uh, um, I drive away."

"Why?"

"Why? Ummmm, I guess 'cuz they figure the dude only wants the cash, so if I drive away…"

"…they've got no one to bargain with, so they just get pissed off and walk away," Aaron finished for him. "It's a good theory, and it might even work part of the time. Maybe even most of the time." He leaned forward and his voice dropped an octave. "But when it doesn't, they'll put a bullet in your messenger's head because they're so pissed off, or because he's already seen their face, or because he already has some cash on him that he took out of the truck."

Mo didn't really have an answer for that. Aaron leaned even further forward.

"So what you need to do is work out with your messenger beforehand what he's okay with you doing. I don't care what company policy is, you ever drive off and leave me standing there with a gun to my head, you better hope I die, otherwise I'm coming for you." He looked at Dave as the new employee's eyes went wide and said cheerfully, "You ready?"

Dave popped the door and jumped down, and by the time he had the door shut again he had his pistol in his hand, per company policy. He kept it down along his leg, walked around the back of the truck, across the sidewalk, and stood with his back against the building next to the front door, looking up and down the street.

A middle-aged man in dirty work clothes approached the bank. He registered the truck, then Dave in uniform standing next to the door, then the pistol in Dave's hand, but all he did was nod as he headed into the lobby. Just another day in Detroit.

Aaron popped the back door, lowered the dolly to the ground with a clank, jumped down, and began stacking boxes of coin. The tendency was to watch the messenger, but the trick was to fight your natural instincts and look away from the target. Dave checked out anybody on foot within fifty feet, any passing car, and even scanned the few second-floor windows nearby, just looking for something out of the ordinary, some disruption in the natural pattern and flow.

"We good?" Aaron was finished with the coin and was about to start with the cash bags.

Dave's head kept moving. "So far." He glanced up at the cab of the truck and saw the new kid watching the two of them, instead of what he should have been, which was everything else. Moron. Nice enough, but not a whole lot going on upstairs.

Past the bank was the parking lot, then another narrow building that at the moment was vacant, and then an alley. Dave saw the squad car as it nosed out of the alley and paused halfway across the sidewalk.

It was a two-man DPD squad car, and both officers were scanning the street. They saw him a second later and he stared back, expressionless, giving them a nod. There was a slight pause, and Dave saw they were taking in the scene—the truck, his and Aaron's uniforms, the dolly stacked with tan canvas cash bags, and the gun in Dave's hand. Then the driver gave him a slight nod in return, and pulled out—heading away from them. Quickly.

"Who dat white boy think he is, standing there with a gun in his hand in *my* city?" Aaron said with a smile, watching the squad car drive away. "We be the po-lice, ain't nobody else should have no guns. Ain't got no respect. Muthafuckin racist, dat's what dat shit is, whitey with a gun, just another perpetration by the man to keep a *brutha* down!" His voice kept getting louder. "Can you dig it? I said, *can you dig it?*"

Dave threw his free hand up in the air. "You know, just 'cause I'm standing here with a gun in my hand doesn't mean I want to get into a gunfight today."

"Relax," Aaron said dismissively. "Man, nobody has a sense of humor anymore. You can't even mention race without being called a racist. Archie Bunker'd get arrested for hate crimes."

"You need some help wheeling that thing in or something?" Dave asked him, glancing up and down the sidewalk. Maybe they'd be able to clear the stop without Aaron causing a race riot.

"Nah, I'm good," Aaron said cheerfully, his voice back to normal. Dave opened the lobby door for him, scanned the interior quickly, then stepped aside for his partner.

"You need to lighten up," Aaron told him as he pushed the heavily laden dolly by. "Have some fun. And I'll give you five bucks if you can figure out what movie I was quoting."

"Seriously? *The Warriors.* Try something hard next time."
"Shit."

Seven minutes later they came back out, Dave in front. He had to step out of the bank onto the sidewalk before he could check left and right, and when his partner didn't get jumped or shot Aaron followed him out with the dolly. He didn't need the dolly as the cash bag, even filled with

$86,000, didn't weigh that much, but Aaron wasn't about to fill both his hands. Keep your gun hand free if at all possible.

Dave stood with his back to the front of the bank and swept the area with his eyes while Aaron rolled the dolly toward the side of the van. The door could be opened by the driver, but neither of them heard a click.

"That moron listening to his iPod again?" Aaron asked.

"Looks like it." Mo hadn't even noticed them come out of the bank yet, he was bobbing his head and staring off down the street. The State Police cruiser was still parked in front of the Coney, the troopers nowhere in sight.

"Jesus, I'm going to shoot him myself before the day is out." He banged the door violently with the flat of his hand. "Pop the door!" he yelled.

Dave used the remote on the garage door but parked in his driveway out front. The Mustang was parked inside the garage on the left side, with about three feet between the car and the wall, which had a small, curtained window. Technically it was a two-and-a-half car garage, but preventing door dings on the 'Stang was a constant battle.

He went into the house through the garage, shutting the overhead door behind him. The canvas lunch bag he tossed onto the island in the kitchen, then hit the switches which flooded the kitchen with light.

The house was quiet, with a few dust motes floating in the air before him. Dave checked his watch and saw that it wasn't even four thirty yet—early day, but that was all for the better. Aaron had been about ready to kill the poor kid by the end of the day's run. He seemed nice, but actually paying attention to his surroundings seemed a little beyond Mo, which is not what you want in an armored car company employee.

"Nice kid, he'll probably be President of the United States some day, but he's not fucking driving for me again," Aaron told Joe back at the vault, never mind that Mo hadn't spent a minute behind the wheel of the truck. His lack of observational skills, an attention span, and his apparent addiction to his iPod had been enough.

"Somebody put you in charge when I went to go take a dump?" Joe asked him, peering through his thick glasses. Dave had just walked away as the arguing commenced.

He grabbed a plastic bottle of Diet Coke out of the refrigerator, took a swig, then headed upstairs to change. Gun, magazines, holster and magazine pouches came off the belt and went onto the bed. It was a big bed, King-size, and he'd made it before going to work. Black uniform belt got hung in the closet on a hook, shoes on the floor in the closet neatly lined up, and the uniform shirt and pants into the hamper.

A fresh pair of jeans came out of one dresser drawer, a black t-shirt out of another. He grabbed the brown reinforced leather belt off the hook in the closet, then the holster and Glock went back on his belt. The double magazine pouch he only carried when he was in uniform for Absolute, and he grabbed a single magazine carrier off the dresser and clipped in onto the belt on his left hip. The other spare mag and the double magazine carrier he left on top of the dresser.

The doors to the other bedrooms on the second floor were open but Dave didn't glance into them as he walked down the hallway and headed downstairs to the big kitchen. The kitchen cabinets were really dated. Had he noticed that before? They might have been original to the house, which was built in '78. Maybe he should paint them, or replace the doors. The appliances weren't that old. He stood there for a while, thinking, then noticed the noise, or lack thereof. The house was really quiet when he was the only person there. A dog would be nice. He'd had a dog growing up, Lacey, but she'd died at the ripe old age of fourteen. But he couldn't get a dog. He was gone too much for a grown dog, never mind a puppy, with all that housetraining. And no fucking way he'd get a cat. Single guy with a cat? Might as well pierce his ears and start wearing pink shirts with popped collars.

No surveillance job tonight, or over the weekend for that matter, so he was on his own until Monday morning. He decided it wasn't too early to eat and dug around in the fridge to see what he had. The leftover pizza he'd save for Saturday...hmmmmmm. Half a steak, already cooked, some lettuce...simple enough. He heated the steak in the microwave while he chopped up some of the lettuce, added a few grape tomatoes and sliced onions. He sliced the steak into thin strips and laid it on the salad, then drenched the whole thing in Italian dressing.

This time of day there was nothing on TV but crappy local news or reality TV court shows. He didn't do reality TV. Ever. "I deal with losers, liars, and idiots all day at work, why would I want to watch them on TV?" he'd said to one of his co-workers recently, and meant it. Daytime TV seemed to be specifically designed to keep losers and morons entertained and distracted from their shitty lives. He grabbed the book he was currently reading, Hemingway's *Green Hills of Africa*, his Diet Coke, and sat down at the small kitchen table by the bay window. When he was done eating, he left the book on the table, bookmark slid into place (not as good as *For Whom the Bell Tolls*, but not bad), rinsed the bowl out in the sink, and put it in the dishwasher. He stood in the big kitchen for a while, leaning against the counter, looking toward the window behind the table but not seeing anything, lost in thought. The house was completely still.

After a few minutes like that he took another swig of Diet Coke, then pulled the cardboard silhouette targets out from behind the couch and hung them on the nails on the mantel above the fireplace. As a kid he used to hang his stocking from them, but that was a long time ago….

He spaced the targets about a yard apart then went back into the kitchen. From the edge of the kitchen to the targets was eight yards exactly. Not as far as he would have liked, but he made do. He unloaded his Glock and placed both the magazine that was in it and the spare on his belt onto the counter, with the round he racked out of the chamber next to them. Then he triple-checked to make sure his pistol was empty. The corner drawer held the weighted dummy magazine and the electronic timer, which he hung on his back pocket.

The timer could be programmed for a random start, and had a par time function with a second beep programmable down to the tenth of a second. Dave checked the par time setting—one second even. Good enough to start. He hit the start button, relaxed his hands at his sides, and waited. Somewhere between three and five seconds later (closer to three this time) the timer beeped and he did a smooth draw of his pistol, getting the front sight settled evenly in the notch of the rear sight and centered on the chest of the center silhouette target, his finger lightly on the trigger, just as the timer beeped a second time.

"Slow *and* sloppy," he muttered to himself. He needed to work on his reloads and shooting on the move, but he started every practice session with the basics, beginning with a flat-footed draw. He took a deep breath, hit the button again, and let his arms hang naturally.

An hour later, his right shoulder and forearm sore and aching, he put the timer and faux magazine away. The spare magazine went back into the carrier on his hip, and he reloaded his Glock and put it back in the Kydex holster on his right hip. Glocks, with their polymer frames, weren't heavy to begin with. Carrying it every day he didn't even notice the weight anymore.

Dave checked his watch. Shit, still barely six o'clock. He peered out the window again, then used his phone to check the weather report, to see if there was any rain rolling in. Nope.

Only a few streets in the square mile subdivision in which his house was located were straight, to deter non-residents from cutting through the neighborhood. Well-maintained sidewalks lined both sides of every street, and as long as there wasn't snow on the ground they were great to jog on.

His four-mile route kept him mostly inside his subdivision and the next one over, with only a brief stretch on a main road. He did a Figure 8 or the infinity symbol depending on how you looked at it. If he was just jogging and not working on his sprinting he normally did eight-minute miles, and much preferred to do them on pavement as opposed to a treadmill. Treadmills didn't work the back of your legs nearly as much. The early evening weather was mild, and in a t-shirt and shorts he didn't break a sweat until he'd done the first mile.

Back at the house he kicked off his shoes and pulled the small Kahr 9mm out of the holster inside the front of his waistband and set it on the coffee table in the family room so he could stretch. He wasn't very flexible, and not likely to ever become so, but knew that if he didn't stretch regularly his chances of injury rose with physical activity. The little pocket auto had a polymer frame and a stainless-steel slide and wasn't likely to rust from his sweat, but he still made sure to wipe it down after every run.

Dave grabbed the remote and scanned the programming guide on the TV to see what was on, then flipped over to HBO. They were doing a *Godfather* marathon in honor of Pacino's birthday, the original and parts 2 and 3 all in a row. Part 3 was mediocre at best, but the first two...it was going to be a good night.

Dave jerked awake and sat up on the couch, not sure why. Something had woken him up, but what? The TV was still on, some Adam Sandler movie, and Dave grabbed the remote and hit mute. He grabbed the Kahr off the table and stood up, checking his watch. After three-thirty in the morning. Late.

The garage door opened and Gina came in as loud as a car crash in her swishy nylon jacket and high heels on the kitchen floor. She looked at Dave rubbing the sleep from his eyes.

"You're here late," he said. He checked his watch again, wondering if he'd read it right half-asleep.

Gina set her big purse on the kitchen counter and looked at what he was wearing, with the TV on behind him. "I was hanging out with Tiffany and Kelly after work. You fall asleep watching TV?" she asked with a smile. She watched him set the gun down as she took off the white thigh-length jacket and hung it over one of the kitchen chairs. Underneath she was in an orange thong bikini above the red shoes, which had four-inch heels. How she could drive in those he had no idea.

"Apparently," he said as she stalked over to him in her tall heels. He could smell the alcohol on her, and the marijuana, when she was six feet away. He blinked a few more times to get his head clear.

"I am so fucking horny," she told him, wrapping her arms around his neck. In the heels she was almost as tall as him, and her chest put his to shame. He wondered if the money he'd spent on health club dues over the years was more or less than what she'd paid her surgeon. She definitely had more to show for it. They kissed, and her tongue was all over his. The taste of alcohol on her was strong. Driving had probably been a very bad decision on her part. He grabbed her curvy ass with both hands and gave both cheeks a quick squeeze.

"I'm a little grungy," he told her. "I went jogging in these clothes, and didn't shower."

She bent her head to the crook of his neck and inhaled deeply. Anyone watching would have seen her nipples harden inside the bikini top. "Perfect," she murmured in his ear, and undid the drawstring of his shorts.

Whorl: Chapter Two

They'd done all the prep work and surveillance that they could, but the day of the thing they always arrived early and got eyes on. The Suburban was parked in a lot across 8 Mile, and they had a good view across the eight lanes of traffic and the grassy median.

Not many cars in the lot they were watching, and the normal amount of traffic on 8 Mile for 11:30 on a Saturday morning. Wilson had shotgun, and looked up and down the border with Detroit through the tinted windows. Nothing looked out of sorts, and there was nothing unusual on the scanner. Not that the lack of concerned radio traffic meant anything, there were always ways for units to keep in touch that didn't involve police channels.

"Fuck, let's *go*," Eddie said from the backseat, squirming. The tension in the car was palpable. Wilson ignored him, as did everyone else. They all had their heads on swivels.

"Anybody got anything?" Wilson finally said.

"Ain't shit," Eddie said.

"I got nuthin, Top," Parker said. Gabe, behind the wheel, just shook his head.

Wilson took a deep breath. "Okay, let's do this. Everybody remember what you're supposed to do, where you're supposed to be. Commo check."

There was a rustling as everybody put their headset mikes over their heads and switched them on. Thirty seconds later they'd verified everybody's equipment was working, and Wilson took another deep breath. His heart was hammering in his chest. Getting too old for this shit.

"Hoods," he told everybody, and pulled the balaclava over his head.

"You know it!" Eddie said.

Gabe, now looking like a bulky ninja behind the wheel, checked to make sure traffic was clear and then pulled out onto 8 Mile. He angled across all four westbound lanes, hit the Michigan left around the median, and waited for a break in the eastbound traffic. When he had one, he powered the Suburban across all the lanes, into the lot, and under the jutting roof.

The valet was in a polo shirt with the club logo on it, and he had almost reached the driver's door when Parker popped open the back door and shoved the AK in his face.

"Shut up and fucking turn around," Parker growled.

"Shit!" the kid said, and froze. Parker was a big man, and muscled the kid, who looked like he was a college student, around to face the club's door. As he marched the kid toward the entrance, one hand clamped around the back of his neck and the AK pointing past his shoulder, Wilson and Eddie closed in behind.

Parker had the kid open the door and they went in quickly. It was dark inside the club, and the shit music was blasting away. Kid Rock, of course.

Splits and Transitions

The bouncer just inside the front door didn't make a peep at the sight of the guns and was swept before them as they hit the main room. Parker shoved the valet away from him and moved left as Wilson and Eddie arrowed ahead.

"Everybody get the fuck down!" Wilson yelled out into the big room, straining to be heard over the country rock. Holy shit did he hate this music. He brandished the AK on its sling, grabbed a man at a nearby booth and pulled him out of it by his shirtfront and threw him on the floor. "This is a fucking robbery. Get on the floor and shut the fuck up."

"Floor! Floor! On the floor!" he heard Parker and Eddie yelling behind him. He kept along the right wall, along the bar, and at muzzle point put about half a dozen customers and dancers on the floor.

The skinny tattooed bartender looked like she didn't know where to go. To get out from behind the bar she would have had to walk away from the man with the gun, and that didn't feel like the best idea to her.

"Climb over," Wilson told her, gesturing with the AK. He then stopped and shouldered the rifle, pointing it at the heart of the man he knew was the floor manager as he stood up from a bar stool. About five ten, with a blonde ponytail, the guy was a serious body builder and probably ran two-fifty, all of it muscle. "We going to have a problem?" Wilson asked him.

"Nope," Shane replied. His hands went up. He was staring at the end of the rifle, and noticing just how steady it was. He had a .380 in his pocket, but one small pistol against three guys with AKs and body armor who looked like they knew what they were doing was a losing proposition. If they were just there to rob the place, fine, they'd never know he had a gun. If they decided to start capping people, that was something different. That happened, he was going down shooting.

"Walk ahead of me," Wilson told him. Shane turned and moved, and Wilson stayed two steps behind him, just out of reach, the AK leveled at his back. *Jesus, this redneck was as wide as he was tall.*

Parker pointed his AK across the room at the DJ in his little elevated booth. "Shut that shit off and get down here!" he shouted. Kid Rock cut off in mid-sentence, and the dancers still frozen on the stages started climbing down awkwardly in their high heels.

Parker stayed by the door and Eddie moved halfway down the bar to cover the middle of the room as Wilson headed for the back.

"Get the fuck out there!" Wilson yelled at the dancers, waitresses, and "shot girls" he encountered cowering in the hallway, one of them still holding the tray of Jell-O shots. *Bunch of skinny white bitches with fake tans, none of them with titties unless they bought 'em, and not one sister.* They sounded like screaming seagulls as they ran past him toward the stage where Eddie was shoving a big drunk guy off a chair onto the floor. Drunk before noon on Saturday. Nice.

Shane stopped in front of the office door. Black steel, it had an electronic eye in the center, and a keypad off to one side. "Open it," Wilson told him.

"—I said get the fuck down! Hey!" Eddie shouted behind him, and the sound of the AK going off was huge. Wilson spun around and immediately saw that the big guy was either too stupid to know what he was supposed to do or too drunk, or he actually might have been trying to put up a fight. Eddie had fired a warning shot into the air, and as Wilson laid eyes on him he saw his partner buttstroke the fatass in the face. He went down then, moaning and bleeding.

"Roo? You got it?" Wilson yelled at him, spinning his head back and forth, keeping an eye on the strip club Hercules in front of him as well as his partner. Eddie had been a bit twitchy lately, and a warning shot was a bullshit amateur move. Now, however, was not the time to lecture him.

"Yeah," Eddie yelled back. He kicked the man, hard, then backed away and swung his AK around the room. The dancers were crying and wailing like they were trying out for an opera.

Wilson turned back to the assistant manager in front of him, and pressed the muzzle of the AK into the back of his neck. "I've got a key right here that can open that door," he said threateningly.

"Yeah yeah yeah," Shane said quickly, and punched his code into the keypad.

"Shut the fuck up!" he heard Eddie yell at the dancers.

"Everybody empty your pockets, and don't make me ask twice," Parker shouted around the club, as the office door swung open. "Cash, cell phones, watches and wallets." Wilson shoved the big man inside. Mr. Utley was in the office, sitting behind the desk, his hands up.

Wilson pointed the AK at the chubby guy behind the desk, wondering just how much his suit cost. Probably thousands of dollars. Well, the guy was worth millions.

"Open the safe," Wilson told him. He gestured at the bodybuilder with the hand not on the pistol grip of the AK. "On the floor." Shane went down without protest.

Utley nodded slowly. "Not a problem," he said, at least pretending to be calm. "We just opened though, you're not going to get much."

"Don't bullshit me," Wilson warned him. "I know you got all your receipts and cash from Friday still. You hold out on me and shit's going to get real painful."

Utley nodded again. "Fair enough. I did hit the alarm, though," he informed the big man standing in his office. Dressed all in black like a SWAT cop, body armor and spare magazines for the rifle bundled around his chest, he took up a lot of space in the small room. Wearing some sort of face mask that left an oval for his eyes, and gloves, he could see the guy was black, but that was it.

"Well then, you'd best be quick about it," Wilson told him. "Bullet holes won't make this place any classier."

Detective John George parked his unmarked unit at the curb on 8 Mile and got out, after first checking the side mirror to make sure no passing car took off his door. Hell, it had happened—not to him, thank God.

On the sidewalk he looked at the club, then looked past it and back behind him. Not near an intersection, no banks nearby, mostly just parking lots…he didn't see any place within two hundred yards which might have a working security camera that covered the club or its parking lot. Par for the course.

COCONUTS. He'd been to a bachelor party here years before, he was pretty sure, although the strip clubs sort of blended together in his head. He wasn't a strip club guy anyway—it was like going out to eat when you're hungry, but only being allowed to smell the food, not eat it. An exercise in self-frustration, far as he was concerned. His life was full of frustration, he didn't need to add any more.

Splits and Transitions

The lot was blocked by a marked unit, with a uniform standing next to it looking bored. George made sure his badge was visible as he walked by the officer but didn't say anything. He was too damn tired, and this was supposed to be his day off.

There had to be a good thirty people inside the club, maybe more, including half a dozen uniforms just standing around eyeballing the strippers, most of whom hadn't bothered to put on any more clothes. At least they'd corralled all the strippers into one corner, out of the way. They did not look happy, like a bunch of wet cats. Actually, they had the same look that he saw on his daughter's face, more often than not. Teenage girls were horrible. Shit, who was he kidding? He'd rather be working than at home, his wife in one ear and his daughter in the other, stereo bitching

"Okay, Rodriguez, what do we have?" He called out to one of the detectives assigned to the task force.

"Same crew," Manny told him. "Unless we have a copycat four-man team, using all the same gear." Two other detectives, Bill Jordan and Ronda Sykes, closed in, waiting for their orders.

"Okay, anybody taken any statements yet?"

"Just started," Sykes told him.

"What was their ride? Same green Tahoe?"

Jordan shook his head. "Black Suburban."

"Shit," George said. "Probably stolen. Well, Bill, once we get the time they rolled in nailed down as tight as possible, I want you to go up and down 8 Mile as far as you have to, see if anybody's security camera caught that thing driving by. Bank, party store, gas station, I don't care. I want a plate."

"Wouldn't that be nice."

George looked around, and up, but the ceiling was painted black. "They got cameras in here?" Yep, there they were. "Anyone take a look at the video?"

"Not yet, Ringo," Ronda told him. "The owner says all the cameras are working, though, so the whole thing should have been caught on tape. Or DVD, or whatever they're recorded on."

"Where are they, in the office? Get in there and sit on them. Right now. I don't want anything getting *accidentally* erased." He waited until she started off. "Anybody know if they were wearing ski masks?"

Jordan looked at his notebook. "I've got two told me ski masks, some others said ninja hoods."

"Shit, let's get these witnesses separated before they start polluting each other's stories. Bill, get those uniforms working on that instead of staring at their tits. We got an owner or a manager?"

"Owner is Craig Utley, he was in his office at the time, and he's still back there as far as I know. Been waiting on you, figured you'd want the honors. Floor manager's that dude right there." He pointed.

"Holy steroids, Batman. Okay, I'm going to talk to him, then the owner. Let me know if you get anything."

George had the guy by maybe an inch or two, but he outweighed the detective by twenty pounds, all of it muscle. Not that George had much muscle of his own…too much coffee, and fast food, and piloting a desk for too many years. He couldn't even remember the last time he'd worked out. And now balding, too, goddammit. Where had the years gone?

"I'm Detective George, the lead on this case," he said to the ponytailed Hulk. "You're the floor manager?"

"Yes sir."

"What's your name?" He dug out his notebook and a pen.

"Shane McDonald. This the same crew that hit The Princess' Diary and Goldfinger's?"

George shook his head. "I don't know. You hear from anybody at the other clubs about what happened when they were hit?"

The big man nodded. "Sure. When the Diary got hit the floor manager Rudy called me up and gave me the low down. I don't know anybody at Goldfinger's, but from what Rudy told me it sure seems like the same crew. Very professional. Body armor, AKs, spare mags, balaclavas, the works."

George looked up from his notebook. "You sound like you know a thing or two about it." How many people even knew what a balaclava was?

Shane smiled. "I know what a fucking AK looks like. Marine Corps. I did two tours in Iraq. These guys knew how to wear their gear, handle their weapons, and work the room. They were moving as a team, they were no gangbangers. Well…"

"What?'

The manager shrugged his huge shoulders. "Well, one of them fired a shot into the ceiling, a warning shot. One of the customers was a little slow to move, get down on the floor. That guy, over there." He pointed out a man getting attended to by one of the fire fighters, looked like he'd been hit in the face with something big and hard.

"And?' The warning shot might mean something. This was the first robbery out of the three where anybody had fired a shot. Or needed to, maybe. At least he knew now this crew wasn't running around with toy guns, or those damn airsoft things that looked just like the real thing.

"And nothing. I didn't see him when he fired the shot, but when I looked over I saw him hit the guy, then it was pretty much over."

"Ummm," George was thinking as he scribbled furiously on his pad. He had a number of questions for the man, and wasn't sure which one to hit first. Where was the shooter standing, what direction was his rifle pointing, how — "Why weren't you looking at him?" he asked the beefy manager. "Guy comes into your club with a rifle, I'd think you'd be looking at him."

"One of the other ones, the leader I think, was walking me back toward Mr. Utley's office. I had an AK pointed at my head and was looking at the office door when he fired."

"Did he shoot straight up? Or—"

"He called him Roo."

"What?"

"The guy who had me, was holding onto me when the other guy fired the shot, he looked back over at him and said, 'Roo, you got it?'"

George lowered his notepad. "'Roo'? Not who, or you, or Lou?"

"No, man, he was the length of a rifle away from me, and I've got good ears. Music was shut off at that point. He called the guy Roo."

Roo? Roo? Shit. He stood there and thought hard for several seconds. "You give your statement to anybody else yet? Any of the uniforms?"

Shane shook his head. "No sir, you're the first person I've talked to."

Oh, boy, this one might have blown wide open, but nobody's going to be happy about it, he thought. "You think this other one, the one who called the other perp 'Roo', was the leader? Tell me about him."

Grab your copy…
vinci-books.com/whorl

Author's Note

As this novel is set in June of 2003, I had to jump in my (not so) Way Back Machine and do a little research. By "research", mostly what I mean is tracking down people smarter or more knowledgeable than me and asking them questions. Or is it "smarter than I"?

See what I mean?

One of those people was Bruce Gray, of Gray Guns, perhaps the preeminent gunsmith of SIG pistols in the universe. I originally wanted John Phault armed with a single-action-only variant of the SIG P226, but a quick check by Bruce showed that SIG didn't begin offering that model until years later. I also had to check with Bill Wilson of Wilson Combat to find out when they acquired Scattergun Technologies and began producing tactical shotguns under the Wilson Combat name.

I have to thank Scott Franz for the name of Bernard Mitton's store. I was talking about the Rush Limbaugh 'Spatula City' parody ad at (of all unlikely places, if you

Author's Note

know me) a small group bible study meeting (circa 2003 in fact). Scott threw out 'The Ottoman Empire' as a perfect name for a furniture store, and it stuck in my head.

In many ways 2003 seems like yesterday, but also a century ago. George W. Bush was still in his first term as President, and we'd just gone into Iraq. *Finding Nemo* was brand new in theaters. No one had even heard the term "smartphone", as the first iPhone was years from being introduced.

I have no idea if, in June 2003, Oakland Community College had unsecured Wi-Fi access. Or Wi-Fi at all. I do know that many businesses and organizations did not, this being the very early years of this technology.

As for the intimate details of working as a private investigator in and around Detroit, in 2003 I was back to doing exactly that, after spending two years working for the Oakland County Sheriff's Department Civil Division serving summonses, subpoenas, and Personal Protection Orders. Every detail of PI work and process serving in this novel comes from my own experience, as do many of the anecdotes. When truth is stranger than fiction, big chunks of your novels can write themselves. Unfortunately, the dog I saw shot in the head by two fools one afternoon in Detroit, and left flopping in the gutter, didn't make it.

Once again, my best editor was my son Barrett, who helped with not just spotting typos but errors in plotting. He read through all but the last few chapters of this book, as I wrote those after he'd shipped off to Ft. Benning to be all that he could be. Exactly what that is I think we're both excited to find out.

Also, as John said in the book, every dog is an emotional support animal. Every dog I've owned in my life has been a rescue, but that works both ways.

Author's Note

Finally, I'd like to thank Stephen Hunter for the kind review of my previous novel, *Dogsoldiers*. It's not often you get to sit and talk writing with someone who won a Pulitzer Prize, much less have them tell you that your book doesn't suck. He's who I want to be when I grow up.

About the Author

James Tarr is a regular contributor to numerous firearms/outdoor publications and has appeared on or hosted numerous shows on The Sportsman Channel cable network including *Handguns and Defensive Weapons* and *Guns & Ammo TV.* He is also the author of fourteen books (and counting), including the critically-acclaimed *Dogsoldiers, Whorl, Bestiarii,* and *Carnivore* (with Dillard Johnson), which was featured on The O'Reilly Factor. He lives in Michigan with his fiancée, two sons and three dogs.